"Why are you so determined to avoid me?"

Gabrielle couldn't see his eyes behind the mirrored glasses, but she knew they were moving over her just the same.

"You haven't answered my question," she said.

Forrester laughed. "And you haven't answered mine." Suddenly his smile faded. "Are you afraid of me, Gabrielle?"

She looked at him in surprise. "Why would I be afraid of you?" she asked quickly.

Too quickly. Even she heard the quaver in her voice.

He nodded. "That's right, Gabrielle. Why would you be?"

SANDRA MARTON says she's always believed in romance. She wrote her first love story when she was nine and fell madly in love at sixteen with the man who is now her husband. Today they live on Long Island, midway between the glitter of Manhattan and the quiet beaches of the Atlantic. Sandra is delighted to be writing the kinds of stories she loves and even happier to find that her readers enjoy them, too.

Books by Sandra Marton

Don't miss any of our special offers. Write to us at the following address for information on our newest releases.

Harlequin Reader Service
P.O. Box 1397, Buffalo, NY 14240
Canadian address: P.O. Box 603,
Fort Erie, Ont. L2A 5X3

SANDRA MARTON

night fires

Harlequin Books

TORONTO • NEW YORK • LONDON
AMSTERDAM • PARIS • SYDNEY • HAMBURG
STOCKHOLM • ATHENS • TOKYO • MILAN

Harlequin Presents first edition March 1991
ISBN 0-373-11347-1

Original hardcover edition published in 1990
by Mills & Boon Limited

NIGHT FIRES

PROLOGUE

RAIN pattered softly against the window of the hotel room as James Forrester pulled aside the curtain and looked out into the grey street. New Orleans in winter, he thought, and a quick smile curved across his mouth, for a moment softening the hard planes of his face. He'd expected heat and humidity; what he'd found was chill and rain.

The curtain fell back and he stretched lazily, his muscled shoulders pushing against the confines of his finely tailored cotton shirt. He looked at the travel clock beside the bed, then at the photograph propped against it. It was grainy, probably taken by a cheap camera, and the edges had begun to curl with handling.

It was the picture of a young woman, taken outdoors at a distance. The camera had captured her as she walked down a city street. Her hair, long and dark, blew across her face, obscuring almost half of it. Her hand was raised before her, as if she'd seen the lurking camera at the last moment and tried to protect herself from its obtrusive eye.

Forrester looked at the clock again. It was time to get moving. She was an early riser—he'd learned that watching her the last few weeks. It had surprised him: somehow, he'd imagined she'd laze away the mornings in that expensive little house of hers in the French Quarter.

He took his suit jacket from the chair and shrugged it on. The soft grey wool was tailored expertly, emphasising his hard, lean body. His glance went to the photo-

graph again, and his eyes narrowed until only the
midnight darkness that outlined the cool blue irises was
visible against his tanned skin. Slowly, almost reluctantly, he picked up the photo and stared at it.

For a moment, he felt as if the woman's defiant eyes
were staring directly into his.

I know you, she seemed to be saying. But she didn't.
She had never seen him—he knew that. A tight smile
twisted across his face as he stared at the picture. It was
he who knew her: her habits, her likes, her dislikes—he
knew everything about Gabrielle Chiari.

His long fingers brushed lightly over the image,
lingering on the full curve of her mouth.

She was so beautiful. She had the face of a madonna,
with eyes that seemed to hint at untold mysteries. There
was an innocent sensuality in the lushness of her body
that brought an ache to his throat.

Forrester drew in his breath. It was all illusion, trickery
captured by the camera and nothing more. The woman
in the snapshot was beautiful, yes, but she was hardly
innocent. Gabrielle Chiari had made headlines back east
only a few months before. Her father had been a small-
time gangster, working for 'Big Tony Vitale', the man
who controlled New York's unions. Vitale had controlled her, as well—until she'd agreed to testify against
him.

He tossed the photo on the table. She hadn't agreed,
he reminded himself, not really. She'd been forced into
it by the federal prosecutor, made to turn State's witness
to keep her ailing father from being subpoenaed. But
John Chiari had died before the case came to trial. And
when he did, when the prosecutor lost his hold on her,
Gabrielle Chiari had fled the city and the protection the
prosecutor's office had afforded her.

Forrester's mouth twisted. She had made her first mistake by being involved with a man like Big Tony, and her second in thinking she could escape him.

And that, Forrester thought, as he opened the door to his hotel room and stepped into the hall, was where he came in.

CHAPTER ONE

GABRIELLE CHIARI paused in the doorway of the converted carriage house and stared into the flagstoned courtyard. Fog, thick as cotton, curled over the old brick walls that separated the house and its outbuildings from the street.

She had lived here for two months, but sometimes it felt more like two years. Gabrielle sighed as she flexed first her right leg and then her left. Would she ever think of New Orleans as home, or would her heart always belong to New York? Crazy as it seemed, she missed the crowded streets and the snarled traffic. Sometimes she even longed to hear the irritated bark of automobile horns and the brusque snarl of a Manhattan taxi-driver.

Gabrielle's mouth twisted. There was no point in thinking about the life she'd left behind. It was over—all of it, the good as well as the bad. Her father had been the good, no matter what the newspapers and the federal prosecutor said, and he was gone. And when he'd died, she'd been able to turn her back on the prosecutor's lies and the agents who'd turned her quiet life upside-down.

She had begun a new life, and, if it didn't quite fit yet, it was only a matter of time before it did. Things were falling into place: the carriage house was beginning to feel like home, the flower shop was doing well, and Alma, the woman she'd hired to assist her, was turning out to be a good friend—even though they were as different as night and day.

Damp tendrils of fog snaked around her legs, bare beneath her running shorts, and she shivered, just as she had every morning since arriving in this city on the Mississippi River. Well, she'd be warm enough by the time she reached the shop—not that Alma would ever believe it. Alma greeted her each morning just as she had the day they'd met. Gabrielle smiled as she remembered.

It had been her first day as the new owner of the little shop just off Jackson Square. She'd jogged to work with a change of clothes tucked into a light backpack, never expecting to be greeted at the locked door by a woman who stared at her outfit in disbelief.

'You must be freezin',' the woman had said in a sweet voice, and then she'd blushed. 'I'm sorry, I shouldn't have said that.'

A customer, Gabrielle had thought eagerly, and then she'd looked down at her bare legs and sweat-soaked shorts, and she'd swallowed.

'Don't apologise,' she'd said quickly, fumbling for her keys. 'It's my fault—I didn't expect anyone to show up this early. If you'd just wait until I change, I'll be happy to help you, Miss...?'

The woman's blush had deepened. 'I'm Alma Harwood, ma'am. I work here—well, I used to work here, when Mr Kastin owned the shop. I was away visitin' when he sold it, and I thought I'd stop by and offer... That is, if you need me. I worked for Mr Kastin for more than ten years, and...'

Gabrielle had almost groaned with relief. Buying the shop had seemed like a wonderful idea—until she'd actually done it, and then the enormity of how little she knew about running a business had turned her knees to jelly.

'Thank goodness,' she'd said, offering her damp hand to the woman. 'Mr Kastin told me about you, Miss Harwood. I tried to reach you all last week—I wanted to ask you to stay on. I'm afraid I don't know as much about flowers as I thought I did.'

Alma had beamed happily. 'I'd be delighted,' she'd said as she put her soft hand into Gabrielle's. Her smile had faltered as their hands met. 'Perhaps you'd better change,' she'd said politely. 'You seem to be—ah—um—perspirin' most freely.'

Gabrielle had smiled. 'Yes, that's a good idea.' She'd started towards the little room at the back of the shop, and then something had made her pause and turn back. 'By the way,' she'd said innocently, 'the word you were looking for is *sweat*.'

Alma Harwood's look of innocence had matched hers. 'Ladies,' she'd said primly, 'never sweat.'

That first encounter had set the tone for their relationship. Separated by age and custom, the ex-New Yorker and the southern belle had found common ground in good-natured teasing.

Not that Alma had been teasing about the freezing mornings. With the blithe ignorance of a northerner, Gabrielle had expected the south to be warm in the winter. But December and January had been cool and grey, with the ever-present fog that rolled in from the Mississippi adding to the chill.

Now it was late February and the mornings were downright cold.

'Don't complain,' Alma had said in her soft drawl when Gabrielle had done just that. 'Soon enough it'll be summer. You haven't lived until you've experienced a New Orleans July.' A look of gentle triumph had flashed across her face. 'I'm afraid you'll have to give up your runnin' come summertime.'

Gabrielle had laughed. 'Sorry, but I'm going to have to disappoint you. I'll just run earlier and sweat harder. You'll never make me into a southern belle, Alma. It's too late. I've been a New Yorker too many years.'

Too many years. The blare of a fog-horn from the river cut through the early morning silence. Gabrielle blinked against the sudden press of tears.

What was the matter with her today? Memories too painful to bear kept crowding in. It was impossible to think about her father's death without a dull ache spreading through her, a dull ache that congealed into a bitter rage.

She had never understood how the federal authorities had found out her father was dying. His illness had come on so quickly that she'd barely had time to grasp the awful truth herself. One week, he'd felt ill, and the next he'd been lying in a hospital room, and somewhere in the middle of all that, while she had still been trying to accept what was happening, Townsend and his men had turned up on her doorstep, like sharks smelling blood in the water.

Testify against Tony Vitale, they said. And when she'd insisted she knew nothing, they'd smiled their predatory smiles and told her she was free to stick to that line, if she liked. It didn't matter to them, they could always subpoena her father and put him on the stand instead.

She shuddered, remembering how she'd pleaded for understanding.

'Please, leave my father alone. Mr Vitale is a union official, and my father is his chauffeur. What could he say that would interest anybody?'

But Townsend had been deaf to her pleas. And eventually, just as he'd predicted, Gabrielle had agreed to testify. She'd have agreed to anything, just to keep the bastards from her father, although why they wanted her to repeat the pointless details of a phone call she'd overhead Tony Vitale make was beyond her. She'd let the men from the prosecutor's office do what they wanted, moving her into what they called a 'safe' apartment, surrounding her with agents—for her protection, they said, which was, she was certain, a lie.

Who would want to hurt her? Certainly not Tony Vitale. No, they wanted to intimidate her and keep her where they could watch her.

It hadn't mattered. Nothing was important, not when compared to her father's illness.

Gabrielle finished the last of her warm-ups, jogged in place for a few seconds, then broke into an easy lope, her running shoes whispering over the uneven flagstones as she moved out of the gate into the early morning streets of the French Quarter.

Running was still new to her. She'd taken it up in the last stages of her father's illness, when it had begun to feel as if her life was bound by the silence of his hospital room and the silence of the heavy-jawed men who were at her side night and day.

Running took you out of yourself, some blandly smiling celebrity on a television talk-show had said one day. By then, Gabrielle had become so cynical that she'd trusted nothing she heard. Still, she'd been desperate enough to test the glib remark. The next morning, she'd put on sneakers, terry shorts and a 'Save the Whales' T-shirt. Then she'd marched into the living-room of the government-owned apartment.

The expressions on the faces of her dark-suited sentinels had been worth seeing.

'I'm going for a run,' she'd said sweetly. 'Does that mean you have to run, too?'

They did, of course, and at first that had been half the pleasure of it—the sight of those pallid, expressionless men panting along beside her in their flannel suits and thick-soled shoes.

After a while, all that mattered was the sense of release she felt while she ran through the city streets.

And it still worked, she thought as she ran lightly along the quiet streets. The morning's run took away the bittersweet remembrances the night always brought. By the time she reached the flower shop, she'd be ready for the day's work, and after that there'd be no time for anything but arranging displays and filling orders and learning the hundred and one things she had yet to learn about the flower business.

Everything that had happened in New York was history. Her father was gone, and the authorities were never going to be able to use her again.

And neither would anybody else.

The streets of the French Quarter were almost empty at this early hour. At night, Le Vieux Carré was thronged with tourists and street performers. Now, the old city showed what Gabrielle thought of as its true face: housewives leaned from balcony windows as they shook out bedclothes, restaurant doors stood open as the old buildings were swept clean.

And the Quarter smelled wonderful. Gabrielle breathed deeply, loving the heady scents of freshly roasted coffee and Creole spices. She teased Alma all the time, telling her she was an inveterate New Yorker and always would be, but the truth was that even she was beginning to fall under the spell of New Orleans' unique charm—not that she'd chosen the city for that reason. In truth, she'd picked it at random, influenced as much by the travel poster at the airline ticket counter as by anything else.

'One-way to New Orleans,' she'd said, and as easily as that she'd left her old life behind.

But the choice had been a good one. The city was different enough to make forgetting the past a possibility. Here, she could escape the notoriety of being the reclusive star witness against the man the papers called 'Big Tony Vitale'. Here, she was not the woman those same papers had eventually hinted was Vitale's beautiful mistress.

It was what the authorities thought, too. She would never forget the way Townsend had looked at her the day after her father's funeral, when she'd announced that she was leaving.

'You can't do that, Miss Chiari. We'll subpoena you.'

'Do whatever you want,' she'd said coldly. 'My father is gone, and you can't threaten me any more.'

'Vitale's not going to let you just walk away, young lady. You know too much.'

'That's ridiculous,' Gabrielle had snapped. 'Mr Vitale isn't a villain. He's been very good to me.'

The sly look on the man's face had enraged her. She'd turned on her heel, knowing she owed no explanations to him, knowing as well she had nothing to fear from the man who'd been like an uncle to her.

Still, when she'd bought her ticket to New Orleans, she'd surprised herself by using her mother's maiden name. No one would be looking for Gabrielle Shelton, a little voice inside her had whispered, and she'd quickly forced it aside, telling herself the reason for the change of name was simple.

Didn't a new start deserve a new name?

Gabrielle's breath rasped in her chest, and she raised her hand and wiped her wrist across her forehead. Of course it did—but that didn't explain why she sometimes awoke in the night to the desperate pounding of her heart, or why she'd avoided making new friends, or why sometimes the sound of footsteps behind her would make her pulse begin to race...

Stop thinking that way, Gabrielle! she told herself. It's nonsense and you know it. Tony Vitale's not the first union official who's been accused of being crooked and he won't be the last. But he's not crooked. Men with power always had enemies, and everybody accused them of...

Damn Townsend and his men for planting such ugly ideas in her head. Gabrielle picked up her pace. She was running harder now, panting a little, but it felt good. The fog was beginning to burn off, and the old buildings and narrow streets of the Quarter were bathed in soft golden sunlight.

She raised her arm and glanced at her watch. It was later than she'd realised. Alma would be at the shop already, waiting with her usual end-of-the-week list of things that had gone wrong.

What would it be this time? There was never anything major—La Vie en Rose was in good repair. It was just that Alma was—Gabrielle searched for the right words—she was perhaps a little too conscientious.

'The roses are dyin', Gabrielle,' she'd say breathlessly, which would turn out to mean that one petal on one rose was turning brown at the edges.

'They delivered the most terrible orchids today,' she'd say, which would probably mean that one orchid was less than perfect.

It had been mouse droppings in the back room last time. As for today—hadn't there been something about the temperature in the refrigerated case being too high? Or was it too low?

Gabrielle sighed. It would take another ten minutes, at least, before she reached the shop. By then, Alma might be wringing her hands in distress.

Just ahead, a narrow alley angled away from the street. It was a shorter route and would cut the time in half. She sighed again, shook her head, and turned towards it.

'OK, Alma,' she murmured softly, 'I'm on my way.'

She had used the alley once before, and she hadn't liked it. For one thing, the pavement was so badly broken that she had to keep looking down. And there was a feeling about the narrow passageway that she disliked, a sense of isolation that was unpleasant. The overhanging balconies, so much a part of the French Quarter, blocked out the sun, adding to the feeling of separation from the rest of the world.

Gabrielle's footsteps faltered as the oppressive brick walls swallowed her up. She grimaced and picked up her pace. There was nothing to be afraid of here. There were sections of the city you didn't walk at all, day or night, and others you avoided after dark, and some of those places were right here, in Le Vieux Carré.

But this shabby, winding alley wasn't one of them. It was dark, it was narrow and spooky. But it was safe.

Her imagination was working overtime, thanks to the dark warnings of the federal prosecutor. Her life wasn't a gangster movie. No one was going to come looking for her or try to hurt her. It was only the government people and the damned reporters who'd bothered her in the first place, both groups chasing blindly after headlines . . .

'Watch it!'

The shouted warning came from the end of the alley. Gabrielle looked up; her mouth opened in a silent scream as she saw the truck barrelling down on her. It was rocking from side to side as it tore through the narrow space, its chrome grill like the snarling mouth of an enraged animal. She saw the workman who'd yelled racing towards her, and then someone bowled into her, wrapped a powerful arm around her, and sent her flying out of the path of the truck and rolling towards the kerb.

The wheels of the speeding vehicle hissed against the pavement inches from her head, and then it was gone, rumbling towards the mouth of the alley, picking up speed as it reached the street.

For a moment, Gabrielle lay stunned. The man who'd thrown her to safety lay beside her, his arm still around her. Her face was pressed into the scratchy wool of his jacket; she felt the racing thud of his heart against hers.

A terror greater than any she'd ever known swept through her and her whole body began to shake.

'Are you all right?'

He was speaking to her. She heard the question, heard the gruffness in his voice, and she wanted to answer, but speech was impossible.

'Are you hurt?' This time, she managed to shake her head. He rose slowly to his feet, drawing her up with him, cradling her against him. 'Are you sure?'

She nodded, then swallowed hard. 'I...I'm all right.' The voice didn't sound like her own; it was high and breathy, but she was grateful she was able to speak at all. 'Really,' she said, more strongly now, 'I'm OK.'

The man's hands slid to her shoulders and he held her from him and stared at her. 'You took quite a fall,' he said.

Gabrielle shook her head. 'I'd rather fall than— than...' The image of the truck roaring down on her came again, and a tremor went through her. 'That truck almost—it almost...'

His fingers bit into her and she winced. 'Yes, it damned well did. What the hell were you doing?'

'Doing?' she repeated dully. 'Why, I was running. I was...'

Her words fell into silence as she looked at the man who'd saved her life. Something cold and hard knotted within her breast. There was an intensity about him that was almost frightening. And his eyes—she couldn't see his eyes. They were hidden behind mirrored sunglasses. Somehow, the glasses lent him a sinister air.

Gabrielle swallowed drily. 'You can let go of me now,' she said, forcing a stiff smile to her lips. 'I'm fine. Really. And I...I'm very sorry about all this.'

A muscle moved beside his mouth. 'Yes,' he said coldly, 'so am I.'

Gabrielle stared at him. If only she could see his eyes, she thought. But all she could see was her own pale reflection.

His grasp tightened and she stumbled as he drew her towards him. 'That truck could have run you down and kept on going,' he said softly. 'Do you know that?'

She felt the blood rush from her face. 'Listen,' she said in a hurried whisper, 'you'd better just get out of here. You'd better——'

'Hey, lady—you OK?'

The gruff voice startled them both. The stranger's hands slid from her shoulders as Gabrielle turned around. The workman who'd shouted the warning to her was staring at her.

She nodded. 'Yes. I'm fine. Thank you for——'

The workman shrugged. 'Thank this guy, not me. He moved pretty fast. If he hadn't knocked you out of the way...'

She looked at the man blankly. He's right, she told herself. This man saved your life, he wasn't threatening you.

The workman cleared his throat. 'I tell that no good Cajun all the time to watch out, I tell him this ain't no raceway, but he don't listen.'

Gabrielle stared at him. 'What do you mean?'

'The kid driving the truck, miss. He's a good boy, he don't mean no harm. Please, you leave him to me. I take care of him.'

The kid driving the truck. The alley, so dark moments before, suddenly seemed flooded with sunshine. Gabrielle threw her head back and laughed.

An accident, she thought; it was just an accident. And of course the man who'd saved her life was upset. Just look at his muddied jacket and his trousers.

She smiled at the workman. 'That's fine with me. You just tell him to be more careful, hmm?' The man touched his hand to his cap and trotted towards the mouth of the alley. Gabrielle turned to her rescuer and stuck out her hand. 'Thank you for what you did. If it hadn't been for you...'

He hesitated, then took her hand in his. 'No problem,' he said easily. 'I'm just glad I was here, Miss—Miss...'

'Shelton. I'm Gabrielle Shelton.' She smiled at him. 'I'm glad you were here, too.'

He laughed softly. 'I'm sorry I had to hit you so hard.' He drew his hand from hers and touched her bare forearm. 'I'm afraid you're going to have a couple of nasty bruises by tomorrow.'

Gabrielle looked at her arm. His fingers were long, the skin tanned, the nails clean and square-cut. Except for the red scrapes and smudges of dirt from the gutter, her flesh seemed pale beneath them. She watched as his hand moved down her arm, then closed around her wrist. For some unaccountable reason, a tremor went through her again. It seemed to take great effort to lift her eyes to his face.

'Bruises are a small price to pay for one's life,' she said.

'You're very lucky, Miss Shelton. It isn't very smart to jog in a place as deserted as this.'

She looked up in surprise. He was still smiling, but it seemed forced. And there was a sudden edge to his voice.

'I don't usually. I was on my way to Jackson Square, and——'

'Anything could have happened.'

Gabrielle's smile faded. 'But it didn't,' she said. She pulled her hand from his and pushed a lock of damp hair from her face. 'Look, it's not that I don't appreciate your concern. But I can take care of myself. I'm tired of being told to be careful. I——'

She broke off in confusion. She'd said more than she'd intended; the look on the stranger's face told her that. Suddenly, to her surprise, he smiled.

'Yes,' he said softly, 'I'll bet you are.' She watched as he lifted his hand and drew off his sunglasses. 'And I can't say I blame you.'

She drew in her breath as their eyes met. She'd never seen eyes the colour of his, she thought as she stared at him. They were a pale blue, like pieces of the spring sky, the irises darkly outlined by a border as black as the pupils.

'You're shaking,' he said suddenly, and she realised with surprise that he was right. He pulled off his grey tweed jacket and draped it around her shoulders, his hands brushing lightly against her.

'I don't really need that,' she said. But she did; she felt the warmth of the jacket as it closed around her. Without realising it, she clasped the lapels and drew the heavy wool fabric around her.

The stranger looped his arm around her shoulders. 'Look,' he said as he began walking her slowly towards the end of the alley, 'we got off to a bad start. Why don't you let me make up for it?' He smiled at her. 'I don't know very much about New Orleans, Miss Shelton, but I do know they brew some great coffee. Why don't I find us a cab? We can go to your home and I'll wait while you shower and change, and then we'll go have some *café au lait* and some of those terrific doughnuts——'

Gabrielle smiled up at him. *'Beignets.'*

The stranger grinned. 'Right. *Beignets*. And then you can show me your city. How does that sound?'

Tempting. It sounded tempting. She had avoided people for so long, afraid that everyone wanted something from her, afraid, too, of nameless things engendered by the mind-games the federal prosecutor had played. And this man was—he was so handsome. No, not handsome really, not in any conventional sense— there was almost too much blatant masculinity in his chiselled features and his well-muscled body.

But Alma was waiting for her at the shop. Besides, she wasn't ready for this. Not yet. Not while she could still think a careless boy was part of a dark plot; not when a stranger's kindness made her suspicious.

They reached the street and Gabrielle paused and looked up at the man beside her. 'Thank you, but I'm afraid I have to say "no". It's a working day for me.'

He smiled, and his eyes moved slowly over her. 'Dressed like that?'

Gabrielle laughed. 'I keep a change of clothes at my flower shop,' she said, 'and I'm late already, Mr—Mr...?'

'Forrester. James Forrester.' A quick smile curved across his mouth. 'How about a raincheck, then?'

She shook her head again. 'Sorry. I—ah, there's a taxi,' she said quickly, raising her hand to call it to the kerb. 'I feel terrible about your jacket and trousers, Mr Forrester. I'm afraid I've ruined them.'

He put his hand on hers as she began to pull his jacket from her shoulders. 'Don't,' he said quickly. 'Keep it, I mean, so you don't catch a chill.'

The touch of his hand blazed through her with the speed and heat of a meteor. Gabrielle stared at him, then swallowed.

'I—I couldn't,' she said softly. She swallowed again, then ran her tongue over her dry lips. 'You don't even know me.'

He smiled. 'I'll come by for it in a day or two.'

Gabrielle swallowed harder. 'It's an expensive jacket,' she said foolishly. 'How can you just——?'

His eyes met hers. 'That's true,' he said softly. 'I guess I'll just have to take something in trade.'

His fingers laced through hers and he moved towards her. Before she could stop him, he bent to her and kissed her, his mouth settling on hers with a gentleness that made her heart stop beating. The ground seemed to shift beneath her feet as she felt the quick, sweet brush of his tongue against her lips.

She heard herself make a soft cry against his mouth and felt herself sway against him. His hand tightened on hers, the press of his fingers almost painful, and then he stepped back and released her.

'Take care of yourself, Gabrielle,' he whispered.

She put her fingers to her mouth, half expecting to feel the heat of his kiss lingering there. Then, before he could say anything more, she snatched open the door to the cab and scrambled inside.

James Forrester bent down, leaned into the driver's half-opened window, and stuffed some bills into the man's hand.

'Take the lady to La Vie en Rose. It's the flower shop around the corner from Jackson Square.'

It was hours later when Gabrielle realised she had never told James Forrester the name of the shop she owned.

CHAPTER TWO

GABRIELLE hung up the telephone, counted to ten slowly, then turned towards the rear of the flower shop. She watched as Alma put the finishing touches to an elaborate centrepiece of long-stemmed roses, ferns, and baby's breath, and then she cleared her throat.

'Is that the last of the altar displays for the Delacroix wedding?'

Her assistant looked up. 'Almost. I've just two more to do, and...' She stared at Gabrielle and shook her head. 'Don't tell me. That was the caterer. Mrs Delacroix's changed her mind again.'

Gabrielle smiled ruefully. 'I'd love to say you're wrong, but...'

Alma sighed and pushed a pale strand of hair from her eyes. 'What is it this time? Are we back to orchids?'

'No, it's still roses. White ones, though. Will we have enough?'

'No. But, if I were you, I wouldn't order any more for an hour or two.' Alma made a face as she began stripping the red roses from the centrepiece. 'That's about how long it'll take Mrs Delacroix to change her mind again. Honestly, Gabrielle, you're goin' to have to learn to put your foot down with these people. If you don't...'

Gabrielle sighed. 'I know,' she said, as she took a vase of white roses from the refrigerated case. 'You're absolutely right. But I'm still trying to expand the business, Alma. Once I've done that, I won't be so easy.'

Her assistant gave her a sideways glance. 'If you were half as tough with Mrs Delacroix as you were with that nice man...'

Gabrielle looked up sharply. 'James Forrester? Has he called again?'

Alma shook her head. 'No. But then, why would he? Three calls in two days, and you haven't returned one of them.'

'I've been busy.'

The other woman sighed. 'I wouldn't be too busy to talk to a man who sounded like that. Is he as handsome as he sounds?'

Gabrielle felt her assistant's inquisitive eyes on her. 'I really didn't notice,' she said sharply. 'The next time he calls, tell him I'm away.'

'He won't believe me, Gaby. As it is, each time I tell him you're busy he knows I'm lyin'. I can tell. I——'

'You're not lying, Alma. I *am* busy. This Delacroix wedding...'

Alma sighed again. 'Honestly, I don't understand why you're avoiding him. He said——'

'I don't care what he said.'

'He said he just wanted to see how you were——'

'This is not China. Saving someone's life doesn't mean you're responsible for that person forever.'

Gabrielle's tone had been sharper than she'd intended, but Alma only smiled.

'Is that what they believe? Seems a nice custom to me.'

Gabrielle blew out her breath. 'Look,' she said patiently, 'I met this man in an alley in the Quarter. It's not as if we were introduced at a party or something.'

Alma snipped off a length of fern. 'He saved your life. I should think that makes up for the lack of a proper introduction.' She looked up. 'Besides, you couldn't have met at a party. You don't go to parties.'

'Alma...'

'Or to dinners or charity function or...'

Gabrielle sighed as she opened the refrigerated case and took out another vase of roses. 'I've been busy. You know that. I'm new here, and——'

'All the more reason to get out and meet people,' her assistant said firmly. 'I have never seen a woman more determined to avoid a social life than you.'

'That's nonsense. I——'

'It's as if you have a fence around you and nobody can get past it. You get that funny look on your face each time someone tries.'

Gabrielle looked up. 'What look?' she demanded.

'*That* look,' Alma said triumphantly. 'The same one you're wearin' now, the one that says, "Stop—don't go any further, I don't want to know you and I'm not about to let you know me".'

A flush rose to Gabrielle's cheeks and she turned away, busying herself with the white roses.

'That's crazy. Just because I'm not a social butterfly...'

Alma sighed. 'A caterpillar's more like it, all wrapped up and hidden from the world.' Her voice softened. 'Whatever happened to you back in New York, to make you so distrustful of people?'

Gabrielle stared at the other woman. What would happen if she told her? What if she said, 'I'm not who you think I am, Alma. I'm Gabrielle Chiari, not Gabrielle Shelton, and I've been used by everyone in the past six months, the authorities and the Press and...'

'You've no reason to dislike Mr Forrester. He saved your life, Gaby.'

He had, yes. But he'd also known the name of her flower shop. Alma would tell her there was a perfectly rational explanation for it, and there probably was. But still...

'Suppose he hadn't been in that alley? Have you thought of that?'

Of course she had. And then she'd wondered why he'd been in the alley in the first place. Tourists didn't frequent such places, not so early in the morning.

Angry tears rose in her eyes. What had Townsend and his people done to her? The world, or her perception of it, had become ugly and twisted. Suddenly, the need to confide in someone was almost overwhelming. Her eyes met Alma's, and it was as if the older woman could read her thoughts. Her pretty face creased in compassion.

'Gaby,' she said softly, 'if you need a friend to talk to, I'm here.'

A friend. Had she ever had one? There'd been acquaintances, yes, girls she'd gone to private school with, and then others she'd worked with. But always there had been a barrier between them.

'Her dad works for Tony Vitale,' she'd once heard a classmate whisper to another. 'Can you believe it? And she seems so nice...'

The youthful voice had been filled with awe, stumbling to silence when Gabrielle had stepped into view. That weekend, at home with her father in the little house they'd shared behind Vitale's bigger one, she'd hesitantly repeated what she'd heard, then asked what it meant. Her father's face had darkened and he'd put his arm around her.

'Your Uncle Tony is a powerful man, Gabriella,' he'd said in his careful, halting English. 'Men such as he are often misunderstood.'

'But—but is he a bad man, Papa? That girl sounded——'

Her father had shaken his head. 'In the old country, no one would ask such a question. Of course he isn't; would his union make him its leader if he were bad?' Her father's expression had softened and he'd hugged her to him. 'Your little friend is only repeating the lies the newspapers print.'

'Gaby?' She blinked as Alma's soft voice brought her back to the little flower shop. 'What is it? You can tell me.'

Can you believe it? And she seems so nice...

Gabrielle drew a shaky breath. 'What I can tell you,' she said with a quick smile, 'is that you're a southerner and I'm a northerner. And if northerners are just naturally suspicious, New Yorkers are positively paranoid.'

An answering smile curved across the other woman's mouth, but her eyes were watchful. 'So I've noticed,' she said. 'But Mr Forrester——'

Gabrielle's smile tilted a little. 'Look, I just don't want to get involved with anybody now. You can understand that, can't you?'

Alma looked at her. 'Because of somethin' that happened to you back home?'

Gabrielle busied herself with the roses. 'You could say that, yes.'

The other woman sighed. 'Gaby,' she said slowly, 'you are goin' to hate me for what I've done.'

'Don't be foolish. Why would I?'

Alma squared her shoulders. 'I told your Mr Forrester to stop by this mornin'.'

'He is not my Mr——' Gabrielle straightened and stared at her assistant. 'You told him what?'

'He said he'd be in the neighbourhood and he asked if you'd be in. So I said——'

'Well, you shouldn't have.' Gabrielle stabbed the rose she was holding into a vase. 'You had no right to do that, dammit! I told you I didn't want to talk to him. Or see him. Or——'

'Good morning, ladies.' Both women spun towards the sound of the amused male voice. James Forrester stood in the open doorway of the shop, a faint smile on his face. 'I hope that's not me you're arguing over.' His smile broadened. 'Although, I have to admit, it's not every day a man has the pleasure of being fought over by two such charming women.'

Alma's cheeks turned bright pink. She giggled and turned to Gabrielle, who was staring at her with icy calm. Her laughter became a cough, and she looked away.

'I...I'll just take these roses into the back,' she said, scooping up the roses and the ferns. 'And I'll call the wholesale florist, and I'll——'

'You do that.' Gabrielle's voice was glacial.

A scattering of ferns drifted in Alma's wake as she hurried to the rear of the shop and the green and blue beaded curtain that separated it from the back room. The beads swung violently as she pushed through, and then subsided.

Gabrielle's heart was racing. How dared Alma do this to her? And how dared this man pursue her in this way?

She drew a deep breath. The last thing she wanted to do was let him see how upset she was. Be calm, she thought, be cool...

She turned slowly and faced him. He was still standing in the doorway, watching her. At least, she assumed he was watching her: he was wearing those damned mirrored sunglasses again, the ones that masked his eyes and his emotions. He was dressed casually, in faded jeans, Reeboks, and a black turtle-neck sweater. A leather flight jacket, well-worn and expensive-looking, hung open over his shoulders.

Is he as handsome as he sounds?

Gabrielle swallowed. 'What are you doing here, Mr Forrester?'

He stepped inside the shop and closed the door behind him. 'And good morning to you, too, Miss Shelton.'

She flushed. 'I asked you a question.'

He grinned. 'I take it you're not happy to see me.'

'Mr Forrester...'

'I'm here to buy flowers,' he said. He smiled. 'Why else would I be here?'

She watched as he began to walk slowly through the shop, pausing every few seconds to peer at a plant or floral display, occasionally bending forward to sniff at a blossom.

'Mr Forrester,' she said finally, 'I am very busy this morning. So if you'd come to the point...'

'What do you call this?' he said, poking his finger at a hanging basket.

Gabrielle looked at the plant and then at him. 'It's a spider plant,' she said. 'And now if you'd just tell me...'

He smiled. 'Descriptive. And this?'

'That's a begonia,' she said impatiently. 'Look, Mr...'

'Roses,' he said triumphantly, pausing beside the red ones Alma had stripped from the wedding display. He looked at Gabrielle and grinned. 'I just wanted to show you I'm not completely ignorant about these things.'

Gabrielle drew in her breath. James Forrester was standing very close to her now; his scent—masculine and musky—filled her nostrils with a dizzying richness.

'I'm very busy,' she said again. She looked pointedly at her watch. 'So if you'd just——'

'Which of these do you prefer?'

She looked at him in bewilderment. He was staring into the case filled with roses and orchids.

'I don't understand.'

Forrester sighed. 'It's a simple question, Miss Shelton. Do you like orchids?' He nodded at the white and lavender blooms in the case. 'Those are orchids, aren't they?'

Gabrielle stared at him. 'Yes. But——'

'Well, which do you like better? The orchids or the roses?'

She looked at him blankly. 'I've never thought about it,' she said after a few seconds. 'The roses, I suppose.'

He nodded. 'Fine. I'll take them.'

'You'll take...?'

'The red roses, Miss Shelton. I'll take all you have.'

A flush spread across her cheeks. 'I have six dozen long-stemmed red roses, Mr Forrester. They were supposed to be for a wedding, but——'

He waved his hand in dismissal. 'Six dozen are fine.'

Gabrielle's flush deepened. 'Save your money,' she said sharply.

James Forrester's eyebrows rose. 'I beg your pardon?'

'I said, save your money, Mr Forrester. The roses will cost you a small fortune.' Her chin rose. 'And they won't mean a damn to me. In fact, I'll throw them away. I'll——'

His eyes glinted with laughter. 'That's a bad business practice, Gabrielle. How can I buy them if you throw them away? Unless...' He leaned back against the wall and folded his arms across his chest. 'You don't think I was buying them for you, do you?'

She stared at him. 'Don't play games, please. You've telephoned a dozen times in two days——'

'Three,' he said.

'—and then you walk in here and buy up all my roses...'

'Why didn't you take my calls, Gabrielle?'

Could her cheeks get any redder? She fought against the desire to touch them with her hands. 'I've been busy. I...'

He smiled suddenly, the kind of smile that suggested they shared a very private joke. 'I thought you might have been trying to avoid me,' he said softly.

Why had she let Alma vanish into the back room? She wasn't good at these games, she never had been, even before she'd learned to question everything a man said or did.

'And that would have distressed me deeply.' The smile came again, flickering across his lips like a shadow. 'You see, you have something I want, Gabrielle.'

His voice was husky and intimate. Gabrielle looked at him, the sudden leap of her pulse reminding her of the feel of his mouth on hers. He laughed softly, as if he knew what she was thinking, and then he leaned away from the wall and began moving towards her.

Her heart lurched wildly. She took a step back; the marble edge of the work-table pressed into her spine.

'No, I don't,' she said throatily, her eyes on his. 'Please, stop this right now. I'll call Alma . . .'

He reached out slowly and put his hand to her cheek. Gabrielle swallowed as he smoothed an errant strand of dark hair behind her ear.

'Of course you do.'

He paused and she looked up at him, trying to seek the meaning of his words in his eyes. But all she could see was the reflection of her own sudden apprehension in his mirrored glasses.

'What do you mean?' Her voice was scratchy. 'I don't . . .'

His lips drew back from his teeth. 'You have my jacket.'

His jacket! She had his jacket! Gabrielle's face registered disbelief, then shock. Of course, how could she have forgotten? But she had: the incident in the alley, his kiss, his knowledge of the name of her shop had all boiled together into a witch's brew of anxiety. She'd stumbled into the shop, gasped out her story to Alma, and tossed his jacket unceremoniously into the supply cupboard in the back room where it still lay, the dirt and grime of the New Orleans street probably now embedded in the soft tweed for eternity.

No wonder the man had phoned so often. He wanted his jacket returned, that was all.

'That jacket's been with me a long time.' He was unsmiling, but he was laughing at her—she could hear it in his voice. 'I'd hate to lose it now.' His eyebrows rose politely. 'Unless, of course, you've developed an attachment to it.'

Gabrielle cleared her throat. 'I'm terribly sorry about this, Mr Forrester. I'm afraid I forgot all about your jacket. I haven't even had it cleaned.'

James Forrester clucked his tongue. 'Terrible way to treat a man's favourite Harris tweed,' he said solemnly.

'Look, I'll take care of it today. I'll send it to the cleaners and...' She turned and snatched up a pad and pencil. 'Just tell me the name of your hotel and I'll have it delivered first thing tomorrow.'

He shook his head. 'I'm afraid that's not good enough, Miss Shelton.'

Gabrielle nodded. He was probably right. After so many days, the jacket was most likely ruined. 'I'll replace it, of course, if the cleaners can't do anything with it.'

Forrester frowned. 'You can't replace it. I told you, that jacket's been with me a long time.'

Gabrielle ran her tongue across her lips. 'I don't know what else I can do.'

A boyish grin spread across his face. 'I do,' he said, and suddenly she knew he'd been leading up to this moment all along. 'You can agree to have lunch with me.'

She drew in her breath. 'What?'

'Lunch, Gabrielle.' She couldn't see his eyes behind the mirrored glasses, but she knew they were moving over her just the same, lingering first on the thrust of her breasts and then on the curve of her hip. 'I suspect you may not have a first-hand acquaintance with the meal, but most people take it at just about this time of day.'

Gabrielle shook her head. 'No,' she said quickly, 'I can't.'

'Can't or won't?'

'Would you mind telling me what this has to do with my returning your jacket?'

'Would you mind telling me why you're so damned determined to avoid me?'

'You haven't answered my question.'

Forrester laughed. 'And you haven't answered mine.' Suddenly, the smile faded from his face. 'Are you afraid of me, Gabrielle?'

She looked at him in surprise. 'Why would I be afraid of you?' she said quickly.

Too quickly. Even she heard the quaver in her voice.

He nodded. 'That's right, Gabrielle. Why would you be?'

'You did come into my life rather unexpectedly, Mr Forrester.'

She hadn't expected to say that; the look on his face told her she'd caught him by surprise, as well. If only she could see his eyes, she thought; if only they weren't hidden behind those damned glasses.

He smiled tightly. 'And it's lucky for you I did, wouldn't you say?'

That was true enough. In her mind's eye, she still saw the truck hurtling through the narrow alley, still felt his arms close around her as he threw her to safety.

'And you knew the name of my shop,' she said, watching him closely now. 'La Vie en Rose, you told the cabby, but I'd never mentioned it to you.'

'You must have forgotten. How else would I——?'

'I don't know,' Gabrielle said sharply. 'That's what I'm asking you.' She drew in her breath, then expelled it. 'And I'd appreciate it if you'd take those sunglasses off.'

His mouth narrowed. There was a silence, and then he reached his hand to the glasses and lifted them from his face.

'Satisfied?'

His voice was silky, his expression taunting. Gabrielle's eyes met his. Yes, she thought, yes, they were that same impossible pale blue she remembered.

They were also completely unreadable.

'Not really.' Gabrielle cleared her throat. 'You still haven't explained how you knew the name of my shop.'

He shrugged his shoulders. 'I suppose I noticed it when I walked around the Square my first evening in New Orleans. I watched the street performers for a while, and then I drifted down some of the side streets. Yours is the only flower shop around here.' He smiled. 'Clever name, La Vie en Rose. But then, I guess that's why you chose it.'

Of course that was the reason she'd chosen it. The former owner had simply called the place Kastin's Florist, and Gabrielle had known instinctively that you needed something catchier than that to make a go of it, a name people would recall.

James Forrester had proved her right. Could she really hold that against him?

'And that alley—what were you doing there?'

He smiled. 'What were *you* doing there, Gabrielle?'

'That's a ridiculous question. I was running. It's a public thoroughfare. You don't need a reason to use it.'

He laughed softly. 'I was walking. It's a public thoroughfare. You don't need a reason to use it.'

She sighed. She'd been joking when she'd told Alma she was paranoid, but that was certainly the way she was beginning to sound. A hesitant smile formed on her lips. 'All right. I suppose I do seem a bit suspicious. But I— I'm new here, you see, and——'

'Don't apologise for being cautious,' he said. She looked at him, surprised at the sudden edge to his voice. 'In today's world, a little caution is a good idea.' He paused. 'But not with me.'

The sheer arrogance of the remark made her laugh. 'And why not, Mr Forrester?'

He put his hand under her chin and tilted her face to his. 'Because I'm the man who saved your life, Gabrielle. Surely that entitles me to a modicum of trust?' A slow smile curved across his face. 'Actually, I'm the one who should be wary of you. After all, you're holding my favourite jacket hostage.'

This time the smile reached his eyes. And it transformed him, Gabrielle thought. His pale, cool irises darkened until they seemed deep enough to fall into; his mouth, so stern and unyielding moments before, softened and reminded her of how warm and gentle it had felt against hers.

She swallowed drily. 'Mr Forrester...'

'James.'

'James,' she said with a little laugh. 'All right, I admit I was a little abrupt——'

'You were. And you were rude.'

'But I didn't mean to be. I'm very grateful for what you did...'

'Then have lunch with me.'

Gabrielle felt the tension seeping from her bones. 'You,' she said, 'are the most persistent man.'

He chuckled. 'I prefer to think of it as "determined".'

'I can't.'

'Is this an example of southern hospitality?' he said. 'What would the Chamber of Commerce think?'

She smiled. 'They'd think you and Alma were working hand in hand. Did she put you up to this?'

James grinned. 'Come on, say you'll come to lunch with me. Take pity on a lonely tourist.'

'I can't. Really, I have work to do.'

'Surely it can wait an hour? My guidebook says you can find the best Creole cooking in town just a couple of blocks from here.'

Lunch, she thought, glancing at him from under her lashes. What would be so terrible about lunch? Somewhere in the background, she heard the phone ring, heard Alma's soft voice answering it.

Alma was right, she had been living a self-contained existence since coming to New Orleans, bruised and battered by her father's death and all that had accompanied it.

But what did any of that have to do with James Forrester? He'd saved her neck, and look how she'd repaid him.

Gabrielle glanced at him again. He was waiting for her answer, watching her with a half-smile on his face. Lunch. Only lunch. That would be harmless enough, wouldn't it?

And yet . . . And yet . . .

Was it her imagination, or was there some darker side to him, something ready to jump out at her the minute she was off guard?

'Come with me,' he said again.

Gabrielle looked at him helplessly. Suddenly, the beaded curtain clattered and Alma poked her head into the shop.

'Sorry,' she said brightly, 'but Mrs Delacroix just called. She says the white roses are out, she wants bird of paradise instead.'

Gabrielle threw up her hands. 'Bird of paradise? What does the woman think I am, a miracle worker?'

'I told her it was impossible, but she insists.' The beads whispered again as Alma drew her head back. Her disembodied voice floated towards Gabrielle and James. 'She says everybody's been usin' roses and she wants something special.'

Gabrielle sighed. 'Poison ivy might be nice.' James chuckled and she turned to him and smiled. 'Well,' she said briskly, 'so much for lunch.'

His eyebrows rose. 'You mean you'd decided to accept my invitation?'

Her eyes slid away from his. 'Yes,' she lied, 'of course. How could I have turned you down?' She raised her head and held her hand out to him. 'Bad luck, I'm afraid.'

His hand closed around hers. 'That all depends on how you look at it.'

She stared at him. 'I don't understand.'

He smiled into her eyes. 'I'd much rather take you to dinner than lunch.'

'No,' she said quickly. 'No, that's impossible.'

'Are you busy this evening?'

'Yes, I mean, no, no, I'm not. But I'll be exhausted after doing the Delacroix job. It'll take all afternoon, and——'

'I promise you a quiet evening, Gabrielle.'

She looked at him helplessly. 'James, really, I can't.'

Her heart tumbled as he lifted her hand to his lips. 'I like the way you say my name,' he whispered, and he pressed his mouth to her palm. 'I'll pick you up at eight.'

'James...'

'Eight o'clock, Gabrielle.' He smiled and folded her fingers over her palm, sealing his kiss inside. 'I'll see you then.' She watched in silence as he walked to the door and opened it. At the last minute, he turned. 'The roses,' he said. She looked at him blankly and he smiled. 'The ones I bought...'

Gabrielle blushed. 'That's OK,' she said quickly, 'forget about them.'

James laughed softly. 'I'm staying at Maison Lillian.' He dug in his pocket, pulled out a stack of notes, and tossed them on the counter beside the cash register. 'That should cover it, I think. Deliver the roses to me there, please.'

'Six dozen red roses? For you?'

But the door had already closed behind him. Gabrielle watched as he vanished into the crowded street. She'd have sworn he'd only bought the roses as a ploy. But then, she'd also have sworn she'd never have agreed to go out with this stranger who'd entered her life so abruptly. The heat of his kiss seemed to burn in her palm. Slowly, Gabrielle opened her hand and stared at it.

He hadn't asked her for her address, she thought suddenly.

Not that it mattered. She had no doubt James Forrester would find her with no difficulty at all.

CHAPTER THREE

GABRIELLE held a pale pink dress against herself and looked into the mirror. The colour was good, it was the perfect foil for her glossy black hair and light olive skin. But perhaps it was too dressy, with its low neckline and pearl-studded belt.

She tossed the dress on the bed and snatched another from the open wardrobe. Too drab, she thought, eyeing her reflection critically. This one was a grey twill, bought when she'd finished business college. The perfect interview dress, her father had called it with a teasing smile when she'd modelled it for him.

'It's important to set the right image,' Gabrielle had said, repeating with earnest conviction the words Miss Mullins had spoken to the school's graduates.

'You do not need to worry about image, Gabriella,' her father had said with a smile. 'I told you, Uncle Tony will give you a job right in his office. He wants you to go see him tomorrow.'

Gabrielle had turned away from her father's smile. 'No,' she'd said sharply, and then she'd swallowed hard. 'I mean, tell him I said thank you very much, but I'd rather find a job for myself.'

Her father had sighed. 'I don't understand you lately, Gabriella. You would not go out on his boat when he invited us last week, you turned him down when he was nice enough to offer to take you to the theatre...'

'I was busy, Papa. I told you that.'

Her father had put his arm around her shoulder. 'I know you're all grown up now, but you will always be a little girl to your Uncle Tony and me.'

'He's not my uncle,' Gabrielle had said, and her father's face had registered surprise.

'He might as well be. He loves you as if you were his own flesh and blood. Why, he's all the family you have, except for me.'

It was true. Gabrielle's mother had died soon after she was born, and there were no other blood relatives. Her earliest memories were of the man she called Uncle Tony. He was always there: she and her father lived in a little house behind his, and she'd grown up as much in his home as in her own.

When she was little, she'd loved to climb on Uncle Tony's knee, laughing as he pretended to pull coins and sweets from her ears and pockets. It was Uncle Tony who had bought her expensive Christmas and birthday gifts, who had paid for her private schooling and the clothes that went with such exclusivity.

'My favourite little niece,' he'd say, and open his heavy arms to her.

It was hard to remember when she had first begun to suspect that Uncle Tony thought of her as something other than his niece, but, during her late teens, his kisses sometimes slipped from her cheek to her mouth, his hands seemed to linger on her a little too long when he greeted her.

She'd told herself it was her imagination. Anything else was insane even to contemplate. Once she'd tried discussing it with her father. But he'd misunderstood her completely. He'd laughed and assured her that she'd never be too old to be hugged and kissed by people who loved her.

People like Uncle Tony.

She tried to tell herself her father was right, that Tony Vitale was just a big man with an equally large exuberance for life. Still, she avoided being alone with him. But she took the job in his office because it pleased her father, and because otherwise there was no way to avoid saying things he didn't want to hear. There was no difficulty: she began in the stenography pool and saw little of Vitale and the other union bosses.

Away from the office, Gabrielle made sure they were never alone. After a while, she began to think that either she'd been wrong about Vitale's interest in her or it had been a passing thing. He went back to treating her with familial cordiality, although there were still moments when she felt his eyes on her.

The charges against Vitale had stunned her. All his employees, not only her father, treated him with respect. And, as leader of a powerful union, he was friend to both politicians and public figures. The walls of his office were hung with photos of himself in the company of mayors, judges, and religious leaders. Never mind what the papers always hinted; surely a man who was a crook wouldn't enjoy such powerful friendships?

His 'friends' fled his side when the charges were brought. Gabrielle had a thousand questions to ask, but of whom? Her father, already showing signs of the illness that would kill him, muttered only that the federal prosecutor was creating a case against Vitale so he could make a name for himself, and then he was too sick to say anything more and she was too worried about him to care. Anyway, Vitale couldn't be a criminal. If he were, what did that make of her father? She'd even said as much to the chief prosecutor, but he'd only laughed.

'Just give your testimony when the time comes, Miss Chiari, and your father won't have to be involved in this at all.'

Her 'testimony' struck her as meaningless. All she'd done was overhear Tony Vitale make a phone call to someone named Frank.

'Riley refuses to come around, Frank,' Vitale had whispered into the receiver. 'I want him taken care of tonight.' His broad face had blanched when he'd looked up and seen her in the doorway. 'What are you doing? How long have you been spying on me?'

Gabrielle had stared at him in amazement. It was the first time he'd ever spoken harshly to her.

'I'm not spying on you! I'm looking for my father.'

Vitale's dark eyes had burned into hers, and then he'd let out his breath and smiled. 'Sure. He's out back, getting the car ready.' His smile had twisted just a little. 'Come give Uncle Tony a big kiss, Gabriella.'

She'd stammered something about being in a hurry and fled his office. Only weeks later, her life had changed forever. The charges against Vitale had made headlines everywhere, her father had fallen ill, and the tabloids, always eager for dirt, had discovered her, the coolly beautiful young woman living in the little house behind Tony Vitale's. And nothing had ever been the same again.

The musical peal of the clock on the bedside table brought Gabrielle back to the present. Her eyes flew to it. Eight o'clock! It was so late. How was that possible?

She stared at the dresses tossed across the bed. It looked as if she'd tried on everything she owned, as if it really mattered how she looked tonight when she and James Forrester went out to dinner.

This wasn't a date. It was a way of saying 'thank you' for what he'd done and 'I'm sorry' for her own foolishness.

Besides, he'd tricked her into this. She'd never intended to go to lunch with him, much less dinner.

Gabrielle looked at the bed again. And yet, she'd spent the afternoon thinking about the evening ahead; she'd been so caught up in her own musings that she'd even managed to be polite to Mrs Delacroix when she'd telephoned for the fifth time.

The doorbell rang and Gabrielle tossed her head impatiently.

'Such nonsense,' she whispered to her reflection. 'Just pick a dress and put it on. An hour of polite conversation in a brightly lit restaurant and it will all be over.'

She reached for the closest dress to hand and slipped it over her head. The doorbell chimed for a second time as she slipped on her high heels. She staggered out of the bedroom, one foot half out of its shoe. 'I'm coming,' she called, and she clattered down the stairs.

She reached the door just as a heavy fist pounded against it. 'For goodness' sake,' she said, flinging the door open, 'don't be so...'

The words died in her throat. James Forrester stood on the narrow porch, bathed in the faint pool of light from the lamp that lit the courtyard. His face was a stone mask.

Gabrielle swallowed. 'I—I'm sorry I kept you waiting. I didn't realise it was so...'

His hands closed on her arms and he half lifted her from her feet as he pushed her back into the house.

'What the hell took you so long?'

His voice was grim and angry. Gabrielle's pulse raced as she felt the bite of his fingers into her flesh. 'What's the matter with you?' she said. 'You're hurting me.'

He glared at her through eyes as hard as ice. 'And what kind of way is that to open the door? Don't you even ask who it is?' Her shoulders hit the wall as he pressed her into the hall. 'This is New Orleans, not some little town painted by Norman Rockwell.'

She looked at him in bewilderment. 'But I knew it was you. It's eight o'clock. And you said——'

'It damned well could have been anybody.' He nodded towards the still-open door as if it were an enemy. 'Why didn't you look through the grille?'

'I suppose I should have. I——'

'Start doing it.'

Gabrielle stared at him. Her heart was still galloping, but anger was replacing fear. Who did James Forrester think he was, anyway?

'I appreciate your concern,' she said coolly. 'But this is my house, not yours. And I do not take orders from you.'

Their eyes met and held. She thought she saw something in the depths of his that chilled her, but it was gone so quickly that later she was sure she'd imagined it.

Drawing in his breath, James lifted his hands from her with exaggerated care. 'Sorry.' He smiled tightly. 'I guess that was a hell of a way to say hello.'

Gabrielle crossed her arms over her chest and rubbed her shoulders. The skin beneath her hands was tender, and she wondered if James's hard grip had left her bruised.

'Yes,' she said warily, 'it certainly was.' She dropped her hands to her hips and tilted her head as she stared at him. 'Do you always come through the door like that?'

His smile grew sheepish. 'Not always.'

Gabrielle nodded. 'Good. Otherwise, your dates would be few and far between.'

The pale blue eyes darkened. 'Is that what this is? A date?'

She felt a wash of colour rise to her cheeks. 'You know what I mean.'

'I was afraid you'd only agreed to see me this evening because you felt you owed me something—or because I didn't give you much choice.'

Her eyes met his. 'Well, that's true, isn't it? You——'

Laughter glinted in his eyes. 'Still, you have to admit my technique's unusual. First I badgered you into having dinner with me and then I made an entrance guaranteed to catch your attention. I mean, you probably expected me to say "You look lovely," or something equally banal when you opened the door.'

She thought of how he'd come forcefully through the door and a faint smile twitched on her lips. He was right, of course. She'd half expected him to show up with the six dozen roses he'd ordered clutched in his arms.

'Something like that,' she admitted

'Well, you were wrong. Even if I hadn't launched into the big city cynic's lecture on household safety, you'd have been disappointed.' His smile was for her alone. 'I could never simply say "you look lovely" to you.'

Gabrielle felt a soft warmth suffuse her skin. She knew what he was doing: he was flirting with her as he had that afternoon. She wanted to say something clever in return, but her tongue seemed stuck to the roof of her mouth.

He drew closer. 'Don't you want to hear what I'd have said instead?'

She hadn't bargained for this. He was supposed to take her to dinner, that was all, and then they could shake hands and she'd wish him a happy vacation and...

He smiled into her eyes. 'I'd have said I was going to have dinner with the most beautiful woman in New Orleans.'

She felt her heartbeat quicken. Say something, you fool, she thought, and finally she did. 'You're right,' she said, striving for a lightness she didn't feel, 'that's certainly not in the same category as the standard "you look lovely" opening.'

His teeth flashed in a smile. 'We aim to please,' he said. 'I like that dress you're wearing.'

Which dress was that? she thought in surprise, glancing down at herself. In the end, she had dressed so quickly that she had no idea what she was wearing.

It was the pink dress, after all. She smiled as she looked up and met James's eyes.

'Thank you. I wasn't sure where we were going, so——'

'I thought we'd dine *chez Gabrielle*.'

She looked at him, eyebrows raised. 'I don't know where that is. But I do like French food...'

James laughed. 'Good. We'll try some another time.' He turned away and stepped out of the door. 'But now tell me how you feel about porterhouse steaks, green salads, and baked Idaho potatoes?'

Gabrielle rose on her toes and tried to see past him. 'I love them. But why would a restaurant with a French name serve——'

She broke off as he turned towards her, smiling at her over an overflowing paper grocery bag.

'My mother taught me to always bring a lady flowers or chocolates,' he said, elbowing the door shut behind him. 'Well, I tried the flowers, but I think I went overboard.' He whisked an old-fashioned nosegay from the bag and presented it to her with a flourish. 'Bet you expected six dozen roses,' he said with a grin.

Gabrielle laughed. 'Something like that,' she admitted, burying her nose in the little bouquet. 'What on earth did you do with them?'

James smiled. 'I made a lot of hotel chambermaids happy women,' he said. 'Which way's the kitchen?'

'Down the hall and to the left.' Gabrielle hurried after him, switching on lights as she went. 'What happened to the chocolates?'

He set the bag down on the counter. 'Nothing happened to them. They stayed in the shop, right where I saw them. After all, what man in his right mind would bring a woman who jogs something as decadent as candy?' He smiled again. 'So I gave up trying and brought dinner instead.'

Gabrielle was still trying to make sense of what was happening. 'Dinner,' she repeated, watching as he began unloading groceries from the bag. 'But I thought...'

'You thought we were going out. Well, I thought so, too. And then I said to myself, come on, Forrester, don't be so pedestrian. Making a reservation at a restaurant is no way to impress a woman.' He slapped a thick package of steaks down beside a head of red-leafed lettuce. 'Cooking her a meal is.'

Gabrielle watched wide-eyed as he added tomatoes and sweet red onions to the stack of foods. A small bottle of tarragon vinegar followed, then an equally small bottle of extra-virgin olive oil.

'Really, James, you shouldn't have...'

'I make the best salad dressing you ever tasted,' he said with a smile. 'But it takes the proper ingredients, so I thought I'd best bring my own.' He took out a bottle of wine and held it up with a flourish. 'How's that?'

Surprise registered on her face as she looked at the label. Gabrielle knew little about wine, except for the Chianti she'd always bought for her father at his request. Amazingly enough, that was the wine James had chosen.

'Perfect,' she said, a little note of pleasure creeping into her voice. 'It would have been my choice, too.'

He looked at her and then bent over the bag again. 'Well, that's good to hear,' he said briskly, and then he pulled out two huge baking potatoes, along with a small container of sour cream and a bunch of chives.

'I don't believe it,' she said slowly. 'You must be a mind reader. I adore chives and sour cream on my potatoes.'

A sudden tightness narrowed James's mouth. He bent over the bag, and when he looked up again it was gone.

'Good,' he said. 'I'm glad I made the right choices.'

Gabrielle smiled as he produced a small pepper mill from the bottom of the bag.

'Incredible,' she said, and then she laughed. 'It's almost as if you know all about me.'

There was a silence, and then James laughed, too. 'Yes,' he said finally, 'it is, isn't it?'

She shook her head as she stared at the small mountain of groceries. 'There's enough there to feed an army.'

James looked at her. 'You don't mind, then?'

Gabrielle hesitated. She *should* mind, she thought. This man she barely knew had tricked her into this dinner engagement; she'd only moments before been assuring herself it would be a quick, impersonal evening, and now here they were, about to have a cosy dinner for two in her own home.

But his smile was engaging. And the feast spread before her was enough to make her mouth water. In this city with its worldwide reputation for world-famous chefs and exotic food, Gabrielle had been existing on frozen dinners supplemented by the occasional hamburger. Somehow, the thought of cooking a whole meal just for herself only made her remember all the more clearly how much she missed her father and the quiet life they'd shared together. And the one time she'd gone out to dinner alone, she'd grudgingly decided that women who felt comfortable dining alone were far braver and more liberated than she.

There was nothing to do but shake her head and give the devil his due.

'No, I don't mind. But if you wanted a home-cooked meal, you should have said so. I'd have been happy to oblige.'

'I wouldn't have thought women like you would even know how to cook.'

The sudden harshness in his voice startled her. She frowned as she looked at him. 'Women like me? What's that supposed to mean?'

His lips drew back from his teeth. 'From what I know of you, I wouldn't think you'd have spent much time in the kitchen.'

Gabrielle shook her head. 'Because I run a business, you mean?'

James drew in his breath. 'Yes,' he said finally. 'Because of that. I hope you have a corkscrew—it's the one thing I forgot to buy.'

'There's one here somewhere,' she said, opening a drawer and poking through it. 'Ah, here it is.' She handed it over and then took two wine goblets from the cabinet. 'I've been looking for an excuse to use these.'

James extracted the cork and tossed it aside. 'Let the wine breathe a while,' he said. 'Hand me that skillet, will you?'

Gabrielle did as he'd asked. She watched as he un-wrapped the steaks and seasoned them. 'Are you a good cook?' she said after a few minutes.

He looked up at her and smiled. 'The best. Are you a good assistant?'

She nodded. 'I know my way around a kitchen.' A shadow flitted across her face. 'Of course, I'm out of practice. I—I don't like cooking for myself. And there's no one to make meals for now...'

'What a pity.' His voice was suddenly callous and she looked up, surprised, but his back was to her. 'What happened?'

Gabrielle pushed aside the spectre of her father's ghost. Tonight was not a night for remembering the bad times, she thought, it was a night for happier things.

'My life changed,' she said with a little shrug.

'I'll bet.' James turned towards her. He was smiling, but there was an unexpected coolness in his eyes. 'It must by very different for you now. Working all day...'

Gabrielle turned on the water and began rinsing lettuce leaves. 'I worked then, too,' she said. 'I've always worked, ever since I finished school.' She glanced at him and smiled. 'Guess what I did?'

His eyes met hers. 'I'd rather not,' he said flatly. 'Suppose you tell me, Gabrielle.'

There was that harsh tone again. Did he think she'd led a pampered life or something?

'I was a stenographer,' she said.

'A stenographer.'

'Yes. Is there something wrong with that?'

James shrugged. 'Nothing, if that's what you wanted.' He stabbed a knife into a tomato and slashed through the red flesh. 'So,' he said finally, 'you worked for this guy by day and cooked for him by night. Sounds like a pretty good deal.'

She looked up sharply. 'I never said that. Where'd you get that idea?'

He looked at her, his face unreadable. 'I just put two and two together,' he said. 'You told me you used to cook for someone and I thought...'

Gabrielle slid from the stool and walked across the kitchen. 'Well, you thought wrong. The man I cooked for was my father.'

'Your father?'

'Yes. But I don't any more. Not since he...since he...' Her voice broke. To her stunned surprise, she felt the sudden burn of tears in her eyes. And that was impossible; she hadn't cried, not even at the funeral. She had been too filled with bitterness.

'Gabrielle.'

She heard James's footsteps behind her. 'I'm all right,' she said stiffly. 'I...'

Tears began to stream down her cheeks. James cursed softly and gathered her into his arms, turning her unyielding body until she faced him.

'Gabrielle,' he whispered, 'I'm sorry.'

'It's not your fault,' she said. 'It's...it's...'

His hand slid beneath her hair and cupped the nape of her neck. She stood rigid within his embrace, her spine like a steel rod, while his hand moved gently against her skin. It had been months since anyone had offered even the simplest show of warmth and kindness to her; the touch of his hand seemed almost a miracle.

She put her hand to her mouth, muffling the first sob, but they came too quickly after that, until finally she gave up fighting and let James draw her into the sheltering curve of his arms.

'I miss him,' she said brokenly. 'He was—he was never sick a day in his life, he was always so strong and healthy, and then one day he just didn't feel well and—and...'

'It's all right,' James murmured. 'It's all right, Gabrielle.'

She closed her eyes, pressing her face against his soft wool jacket. 'Sometimes, I still don't believe he's gone. I just—I just...' Her tears, so long repressed, seemed unstoppable. 'He was all I had.'

His arms tightened around her. 'Was he?'

Later, it would seem a strange question. Now, it made perfect sense. Gabrielle nodded and sniffed damply. 'And they said such terrible things about him, James. None of it was true. None of it. I...'

She fell silent. What was the matter with her? She was talking too much, saying things she couldn't afford to say, not if she was to maintain her new identity. This morning, she'd been filled with doubts about James Forrester. Now she was babbling to him, on the verge of spilling secrets that had to remain locked within her forever if she was to have any peace.

She was Gabrielle Shelton, not Gabrielle Chiari. She could never be Gabrielle Chiari again.

She wiped her hand across her nose and stepped back in James's arms. Her tears had left dark spots on his jacket.

'I seem to make a specialty out of ruining your clothing,' she said, forcing a smile to her lips. 'Let me get a tissue before I do any more damage.'

He kept one arm around her while he reached in his pocket and drew out a handkerchief. 'Here you go,' he said, holding it out to her. 'Use this.'

Gabrielle shook her head. 'I couldn't.' She laughed through the tears that still trickled down her face. 'My mascara's running. I'll ruin your handkerchief.'

James smiled at her. 'What's a handkerchief, compared to two wool jackets and a pair of trousers? Go on, I'll risk it.'

She laughed again, wiped the tears from her eyes, then blew her nose loudly. 'Thank you.'

He nodded solemnly. 'You're welcome. I think you needed that cry.'

Gabrielle sighed. 'I think you're right.' She dabbed at her eyes again. 'You know what else I need?'

Their eyes met. 'Yes,' he said softly, and, before she could move, he cupped her face in his hands and kissed her.

The kiss was gentle, but the feel of his mouth against hers was electric. James made a sound deep in his throat, and gathered her to him, his lips parting hers so he could taste her. For a second, she swayed against him, and then she put her hands against his chest and drew away.

'That's not quite what I had in mind,' she said. She'd been trying for a light tone, but her voice sounded hoarse and uncertain.

'Gabrielle...'

'If you don't feed me soon, I swear I'm going to swoon.'

A smile touched his lips, but she could feel the racing beat of his heart beneath her palms. 'Is that what happens when you live in the south? Do you learn to swoon?'

She laughed softly. 'Alma says that went out with Scarlett O'Hara. If I faint, you'll have nothing but low blood-sugar to blame.'

He touched the tip of her nose with his finger. 'Can I trust you to make the salad?'

Gabrielle nodded. 'Of course. Can I trust you to grill the steaks?'

James laughed. 'You'll eat those words, young lady.'

She smiled. 'I'd rather eat the steaks.'

James was a quick and efficient cook. He worked with his jacket off and his shirt-sleeves rolled up, and there was something very masculine in the way he moved around her small kitchen. They dined before the fire-place by candle-light, talking about a lot of things, none of them terribly important.

What was important, Gabrielle thought, as she watched James from beneath her lashes, was that she was happy. It was a feeling she'd almost forgotten.

And when the evening ended, when he took her in his arms and whispered goodnight, she trembled, eyes closed, awaiting his kiss. His mouth moved against hers as lightly as the touch of spring rain against a petal, and then he drew back and looked at her.

'Gabrielle,' he whispered.

Her lashes lifted and her eyes met his. He was watching her with an intensity that made her breath catch.

'Gabrielle,' he said again, and the single word seemed to hold a complexity of meaning.

'What is it, James? Is something wrong?'

His eyes grew dark, his hands spread along her shoulders, and suddenly he drew her to him and kissed her with a passion that sent heat spiralling through her blood.

Time slowed, then stopped. She stood motionless while James's mouth moved on hers, and then she whimpered and rose on tiptoe, her body straining to press against his. Her arms lifted and wound tightly around his neck.

With a soft groan, he caught her wrists, drew her hands to her sides and then thrust her from him.

'Lock the door after me,' he said in a rough voice, and before she could answer he was gone.

Gabrielle awoke abruptly in the middle of the night, her heart pounding, her skin clammy with sweat. She had been dreaming of James—already, the dream images were fragmented and illusory. One thing, however, was all too clear.

She had lived carefully, almost reclusively, for months, and now, in little more than a day, a stranger had entered her life, a man who seemed to know all kinds of little things about her, whose embrace breached all her defences.

Alma would say it was wonderful, a sure sign of romance in an otherwise humdrum world.

But was it?

CHAPTER FOUR

'WHY would anybody in his right mind give house-room to one of these things?' Alma made a face as she plucked a tiny cactus spine from the tip of her finger. 'I declare, these thorny devils bite the hand that feeds them!'

Gabrielle, seated opposite her assistant at the small work-table in the rear room of the La Vie en Rose, looked up and smiled.

'You have to learn to appreciate succulents,' she said. 'After all, they have a lot going for them.'

Alma's eyebrows rose. 'Besides their propensity for blood-lettin' you mean?'

Gabrielle laughed. 'Give credit where credit's due, Alma. Cacti are tough, they don't need much care or looking after...'

'Everythin' needs some care, Gaby.' The other woman's eyes narrowed in speculation. 'And even the thorniest exterior can mask a tender heart.'

The two women looked at each other for a silent moment, and then Gabrielle's cheeks turned pink and she pulled a box of ribbons and bows towards her.

'Red or white?' she asked. Alma said nothing, and Gabrielle looked up. 'What do you think—shall I use red or white ribbon for these carnation corsages?'

'Red,' Alma said, 'and don't try to change the subject.'

Gabrielle bent forward again. Her hair, held back at the temples with tortoiseshell combs, swung forward and hid her face behind a glossy black curtain.

'Did you want to talk about cacti?' she said in tones of absolute innocence. 'I didn't realise that. Actually, I don't know much about them, except that they're hardy and self-sufficient——'

'Darn it!' Alma tossed down the miniature trowel she was holding and stuffed her finger into her mouth. 'There's also not a thing about them anyone can admire, except for the fact that they don't need much water.' Her dark brown eyes glittered. 'But then, neither do camels—although I suppose even a camel admires another camel some time, or there wouldn't be any more camels, would there?'

Gabrielle raised her head and the two women stared at each other, until finally she sighed wearily. 'All right,' she said, pushing aside the bows and ribbons she'd scattered on the table, 'let's get to it, shall we?'

'Get to what? I was simply talkin' about——'

'Cacti and camels,' Gabrielle said drily, 'yes, I know.' Her green eyes fixed on her assistant. 'Is that what you think I am, Alma? A cactus?'

Alma's cheeks flushed. 'I think it's what you pretend to be—you know, all thorns and toughness on the outside.' She took a breath. 'But what I said before is true, too. Even a cactus needs care if it's goin' to flower.'

Gabrielle sighed and wiped her hands on her smock. 'OK, cacti need care and...'

Alma put her elbows on the table and propped her face in her hands. 'And for starters, you look awful.'

'Thank you. That's always nice to hear.'

'You have dark circles under your eyes,' Alma said with dogged determination.

Gabrielle looked away. 'I didn't sleep well last night.'

'And each time that phone rings, you look at it as if you're afraid it's going to bite you.'

'That's not so. I'm just hoping we don't get many more orders. I'm pleased we've had so many, but with *mardi gras* coming on and all these private balls...'

'It's the calls from James you're worried about. Each time I tell you it's him, you get this panicked look on your face and you shake your head.'

'I haven't time for private calls. These orders...'

'Gaby, I wasn't born yesterday. How can you refuse to take his calls when you care for him?'

'Care for him?' Gabrielle gave a forced laugh. 'I barely know him.'

'Well, you could remedy that easily enough. You could——'

'Alma.' Gabrielle's voice was caustic. 'You're making more out of this than it deserves. James Forrester is in New Orleans on a visit—he'll be gone in a few days, but I'll still be here and so will this shop. I suggest we put our efforts into it and not into daydreams about romance with a stranger.'

'How many days?'

Gabrielle looked at her friend blankly. 'How many days what?'

Alma sighed. 'You said he'd be gone in a few days and I just wondered how many? Did he say last night?'

Gabrielle shook her head. 'What does it matter? Soon he'll go back to wherever he came from, and——'

'Where's that?' Alma shook her head and sighed at the puzzled expression on her employer's face. 'Where does he come from? Did he say?'

'No. Actually, we didn't talk about him at all.'

'What did you talk about, then?'

Gabrielle looked at her. 'Nothing very special. Just—just things. Music. Politics. This and that.'

'Dull stuff, hmm? Well, no wonder you don't want to see the man again.'

'It wasn't dull at all,' Gabrielle said quickly. 'I really enjoyed it. We...' The sly grin on Alma's face brought her to a stumbling halt. 'I don't know what that's supposed to prove. I never claimed we didn't have a pleasant evening. But...'

'But what?' Alma made a face. 'Don't tell me. He eats with his hands.'

'No, of course he doesn't.'

'You got all dressed up and he took you to McDonald's.'

Gabrielle smiled. 'Stop being silly.'

'Where did he take you, then? Some place romantic, I hope.'

'Actually, we ate in. James brought dinner with him.'

Alma's eyebrows rose. 'I didn't know Antoine's catered.'

Gabrielle shook her head. 'He brought steak and all the trimmings. Even wine. And he did all the cooking.' Her eyes darkened as she remembered. 'We ate in front of the fireplace. It was—it was . . .'

'What? Awful? Did he burn the steak?'

Gabrielle laughed. 'No.'

'Then what's the problem? I know—you're a closet health nut. The foolish man brought beef and the evil fermented grape, and you'd have preferred tofu and goat's milk.'

Again, laughter bubbled in Gabrielle's throat. 'In fact, he chose all my favourite things. It was all . . .' Her laughter faded and she looked sharply at Alma. 'You didn't tell him anything, did you? I mean, did he ask you what I liked?'

The expression on Alma's face was answer enough. 'Me? I never had two minutes alone with the man.' She smiled. 'Sounds like a perfect date so far. What did you do after dinner? Did you go out to a film or somethin'?'

'I told you, we sat and talked. James built a fire and we had coffee . . .'

Her voice drifted away. Alma cleared her throat in the silence. 'Well,' she said carefully, 'that certainly explains why you don't want to see him again. After all, there's just so much a woman can take. Who'd want to

spend an evenin' like that too often? You might begin
to like it, and then what would you do?'

Gabrielle sighed deeply. 'All right, I admit it—I had
a good time.'

Alma's eyes sought hers. 'Which is why you don't want
to talk to him today,' she said with dry understatement.

Gabrielle looked at her. She knew what was behind
Alma's taunt. Her assistant had once gently described
her as a shy violet, hiding from the real world in the
safety of a dark wood.

If only it were that simple, she thought.

The shrill ring of the telephone made her start. Both
women looked at the instrument and then at each other.

'Well?' Alma's voice was soft. 'Will you answer it, or
are we back to playin' games?'

Gabrielle stared at the phone again and then she turned
away. 'You get it,' she said briskly. 'I'm going to see if
we have any more bud vases in the front cupboard.'

'Gaby——'

'I'll be back in a minute.'

'Gaby—if it's James callin'...'

Gabrielle paused in the doorway. 'Tell him—tell
him...' She swallowed. 'Tell him I'm out.'

The beaded curtain clattered as she moved through it
into the shop's showroom. Alma's voice droned softly
behind her, and she found herself straining to hear what
her assistant was saying. The realisation that she was
doing that was disquieting.

What did it matter if it was James or not? He'd called
half a dozen times this morning, and he'd probably call
that many times this afternoon, and she still wasn't about
to change her mind.

She wasn't going to take his calls, and she certainly
wasn't going to see him again. Last night had been the
first and last date she and James Forrester would ever
have.

Gabrielle walked to the front window and looked out. It had rained all through the night and it was still raining, although Alma kept promising that the sun would break through the clouds soon.

'It's always nice for *mardi gras*,' she'd said with conviction as Gabrielle stood dripping just inside the door that morning.

Not that it would matter much. Rain or no, the elaborate balls that preceded Shrove Tuesday would go on, and the little shop had already taken more orders than she'd dreamed possible. Business would be fine, no matter what the weather.

As for her own state of mind—she sighed and turned away from the window. The weather couldn't affect that at all. Her melancholy mood hadn't come from grey skies. It was a mood of the heart, not of the barometer.

A flash of red in the refrigerated case caught her eye. Red roses, and the memory of yesterday morning when James had bought all six dozen in the shop, brought a bittersweet smile to her mouth. Bringing her that little bouquet instead of the roses had only been one of an endless series of surprises.

During the sleepless night, she'd remembered another man who'd surprised her once. She'd been coming out of her father's hospital room, swaying with exhaustion, and a man in a white coat had asked, compassionately, if she'd like to have a cup of tea. It had been months since anyone had offered her anything without wanting something in exchange, and she'd stopped and stared at him.

'It will do you good, Miss Chiari,' he'd said, and she'd let him lead her halfway to the cafeteria before she'd spotted the tape recorder in his pocket and realised he was a reporter whose concept of compassion only involved himself.

The thought that James was a reporter had occurred to her during the long night. But she'd dismissed it quickly. There was a hardness about him, a sense of self that told her he could never spend his time scurrying after meaningless stories. Besides, he hadn't tried to steer the conversation to New York or Tony Vitale, or anything remotely connected with the life she'd left behind.

She'd stared into the darkness of her bedroom, trying to make sense of the past few days. Finally, she'd pushed aside the tangle of sweaty blankets, slipped on her robe and padded down to the kitchen, thinking that perhaps a glass of warm milk would help.

Had James's entry into her life really been accidental? Her tired brain replayed the incident in the alley over and over again. And he seemed to know so much about her—was that coincidence, too, or was there some darker reason?

She knew those were questions no woman in her right mind would ask. Who wouldn't want to meet a handsome, exciting man who first saved your life and then seemed to anticipate your every desire?

Gabrielle had filled a pan with milk and put it on the stove.

There wouldn't have been any doubts a year ago. 'My innocent Gabriella,' her father had called her once, and she knew it was true. She'd led a sheltered life. The Vitale compound was quiet and secure, and insulated from the world.

In the real world, people were not always what they seemed. The authorities who were sworn to uphold the law hadn't hesitated to coerce her into co-operating. Reporters had lied to get her story. And the man she called Uncle Tony was...

Was what? A union boss, that was all he was.

Suppose—just suppose there was more to it than that. Suppose there was substance to the ugly charges levelled against him. Suppose her testimony, simple as it was, might damage him.

Vitale's not going to let you just walk away, young lady...

The milk had hissed as it boiled over the rim of the pan, and she'd snatched it from the stove, drawing in her breath as the pot handle burned her fingers.

No. That was ridiculous. Uncle Tony wasn't—he wouldn't...

Besides, if James had been sent to hurt her, he could have just let the truck run her down that first morning. And they'd been alone for hours last night.

Unless he was toying with her. Or waiting for his orders. Or...

Gabrielle drew in her breath. The past months had turned her brain to mush. She wasn't in any danger, not from Tony Vitale. It was the authorities who'd turned her life upside-down, not he.

The rain had lessened by morning. She'd put on a sweatsuit and her running shoes and started towards the shop. She had almost been there when thunder rolled across the sky and the rain turned into a downpour. Gabrielle had lifted her face to the drops and let them cool her flushed cheeks. Suddenly, what had happened with James had seemed very simple to understand.

He didn't really know anything about her. Steaks, baked potatoes and green salads were standard American fare, red wine and the little bouquet of flowers were charming romantic touches.

Her cynical reaction to the evening was what didn't fit the picture. She'd been riding an emotional roller-coaster for so long that it had twisted her view of life.

Her past was still with her, and until she managed to put it aside, until she could look at life without seeing shadows where there were none, the best kind of relationship was no relationship at all, and never mind the way her body had seemed to turn to warm honey in James's arms.

'Gaby?'

She turned, startled, as Alma stepped through the beaded curtain, her pretty face wreathed in frowns.

Gabrielle sighed. 'Don't tell me. The cactus plants have decided to mount all-out war and...' Her teasing words drifted to silence. 'Alma? What's happened?'

The other woman swallowed. 'It's—it's the hospital, Gaby. They asked for you.'

Gabrielle's mouth went dry. Wispy memories rose like smoke from a dying fire; she felt herself spinning back to a time when a call from the hospital could only be a harbinger of tragedy.

She brushed past Alma and pushed through the curtain. Her hand shook as she snatched up the telephone.

'This is Gabrielle Shelton,' she said.

The disembodied voice was the same as the ones she'd heard so many times before—cool, efficient, and determined to give nothing away.

'Ms Shelton, this is St Francis Hospital. Do you know a James Forrester?'

No. *No!*

Gabrielle sank back against the door-jamb. 'Yes, yes, I know him.'

'There's been an accident, Ms Shelton.'

'An accident?'

'An automobile accident. Mr Forrester had your name and phone number on his person. We thought, if you were a friend or a relative...?'

There was a questioning silence. 'No, I'm not. Not really. I...' She drew a deep breath. 'Is he...is he...?'

'The doctor is with him now. I'm afraid you'll have to ask your questions of him.'

'But I'm not...'

Gabrielle closed her eyes. She remembered how lonely a place a hospital could be, how little human warmth there was amid all the life-saving machinery.

More than that, she remembered the way she'd felt when James had held her, the slow heat that had penetrated the thorny exterior within which she hid. Suddenly, the decisions of a moment ago were meaningless.

She grabbed for her coat, then pulled a notepad towards her.

'Tell me how to get there,' she said.

Seconds later, Gabrielle flew out of the door.

CHAPTER FIVE

WHY was traffic always at its worst when you were in a hurry? Rain drummed against the windscreen of Gabrielle's little Toyota as she sat waiting for a traffic light to change. She glanced at the clock on the dashboard, then slapped her hand on the steering-wheel.

'Come on, come on,' she muttered.

The light turned to green and Gabrielle stepped on the accelerator. The car dashed through the intersection, skidding lightly as she turned down Bienville Road. She had to be close to the hospital by now—the woman on the phone had given clear directions. Of course, she hadn't written them down half as clearly. Apprehension had made her handwriting suddenly cramped and spidery. But surely she'd followed all the rights and lefts and...?

Yes! There it was, St Francis Hospital, an old red-brick building rising out of the mist. Her heart thudded as she pulled into the car park and found a space for the Toyota. Soon, she thought, stepping out into the rain, soon she'd know.

She'd tried not to think about what awaited her while she drove. Experience had taught her that that kind of speculating only made things worse. But by the time she'd got halfway across the city, a cold knot of anxiety lay heavy in her breast. Please, she'd kept thinking, please.

The hospital lobby was like an aquarium tank. Rain drummed against the windows and washed down the glass. Bright lights cast unrelenting illumination on the cold plastic furnishings.

Gabrielle's footsteps faltered as she neared the information desk. Please, she thought, please...

The receptionist's smile was as false as her hair colour. 'Yes? May I help you?'

Gabrielle cleared her throat. 'James Forrester,' she said in a papery whisper. 'I—I had a call about him a little while ago. I wondered if you could—if you knew...'

'Regular or Emergency?'

'I don't...'

'Did he come in through Regular Admissions or Emergency?'

'I don't know. They said—they said he'd had an automobile accident.'

The receptionist nodded. 'Emergency, probably. Go straight down that hall and then turn left. You can't miss it.'

Her heart was racing by the time she reached the swinging doors that led to the emergency clinic. Easy, she told herself, easy. She took a last deep breath and then pushed open the doors.

The sights and smells of the clinic rolled over her like a wave against a sandy beach. Memories rushed back and an all-too familiar nausea rose in her throat. She swallowed past it, then swallowed again until she'd conquered it.

Easy does it, she told herself. You'll be no use at all if you let this happen.

She moved slowly into the room, breathing shallowly, trying to ignore the feeling of *deja vu* that accompanied being in a hospital again. James had to be here somewhere—the only question was how to find him. That was what she'd concentrate on.

The room was overflowing with people and noise. Babies wailed in their mothers' arms; the melodic chimes of an electronic pager insisted on being heard. Voices rose and fell, the soft sounds of the south mingling with the strangely strident tones of downtown New Orleans.

Gabrielle's nostrils flared at the sting of the pungent antiseptic, rejecting the darker smells she knew lay just beneath.

Ordered lines of metal chairs faced another admission desk. A woman seated in one of the chairs looked up, her eyes dark with exhaustion. Beside her, a man coughed apologetically into his handkerchief.

Gabrielle's gaze swept past them, still searching for James. There was a double-width doorway beyond the chairs, through which she glimpsed examination cubicles, and she took a hesitant step in that direction.

'Out of the way, miss. Comin' through.'

She scrambled back as a gurney trundled by. A sheet-covered figure lay on it, face turned aside, bottles and tubes snaking from beneath the sheet.

Gabrielle's legs turned to jelly. 'James?' she whispered.

The face turned to her and she breathed a sigh of relief. No. Not James, thank God. Not . . .

'Gabrielle?'

The voice was low, tight with exhaustion, but she knew it at once.

'James,' she whispered, spinning towards the sound.

All the doubts she'd harboured about him such a short time ago fell from her like petals from a flower. He looked the way he sounded—weary, in pain, almost defeated. He was sitting on a metal chair, his left leg stiffly elevated on a low stool. His trousers were ripped to the knee; she glimpsed tape or plaster, white as bone, lying just beneath. A pair of crutches leaned against the wall beside him.

A feeling of anguish swept through her, followed by a relief so intense that it made her dizzy. He'd been injured, but he was all right. A smile lit her face.

An answering smile curved across his mouth as she hurried towards him, but it only accentuated the weariness that lay stretched over his face like a mask.

Her smile dimmed as she drew nearer. It wasn't just his leg that was injured. A delicate tracery of stitches angled high across one cheek to vanish in his dark hair, and there was a bruise the colour of a storm-cloud along his jaw. He looked awful, she thought with a swift intake of breath, and it took monumental effort to keep even a remnant of the smile on her face.

'Thank you for coming, Gabrielle.' His mouth twisted. 'I didn't ask them to call you. I had no idea until they told me——'

She shook her head, cutting off his apology. 'Never mind that,' she said. 'Are you all right? They wouldn't tell me anything on the phone.'

'I'm just fine,' he said, smiling, and then his smile turned into a grimace as he shifted his leg. 'It's the car that's wrecked. I'm afraid I'm not going to be one of Hertz's favourite customers after they get a look at their Ford.'

'What happened?' Her eyes moved over him, coming to rest on his leg. 'Is it—did you . . . ?'

James sighed. 'My fault entirely. I was going too fast and I took a corner too quickly. The car ended up with its nose tucked into a telephone pole.' He grimaced again and cupped his hand over his knee. 'And my knee ended up in the dashboard,' he said with a wry smile. 'They tell me that wasn't the best place for it, especially since I'd already done a number on it playing college football years ago.'

'It's not broken, then?'

'No, no broken bones. I was lucky.'

Relief swept through her again, this time followed by annoyance at herself that he should matter so much to her. It sharpened her tongue when she spoke.

'Why is it that grown men think they have to prove themselves by driving too fast? Of course you were lucky—but they say God watches out for drunkards and fools.'

James's eyes narrowed. 'OK,' he said tightly, 'I suppose it was dumb. But I'd made up my mind that I wasn't going to have a pointless chat with your assistant.'

'I don't understand.'

'It isn't very complicated. As charming as the lady is, I'd run out of things to say to Miss Harwood.' His breath hissed between his teeth as he moved his leg again. 'I decided the only way I was going to talk to you was by catching you in your shop.'

His words tore into her. 'I don't know what you mean,' she said, but she did, and her guilt was sharp as a knife-edge.

His eyes narrowed. 'You did get my messages, didn't you?'

She swallowed. 'Yes.'

He nodded. 'Are you going to tell me why you refused my calls?'

She stared at him helplessly. How could she tell him the truth? She couldn't; she wasn't even sure what the truth was.

'I—I was busy. Didn't Alma tell you? We've been very lucky, taking lots of orders for *mardi gras* balls and dinners and...'

James lowered his leg to the floor and twisted towards the crutches. 'Come on, Gabrielle, I wasn't born yesterday.'

His voice was rough, and she thought it was irritation until she saw the sudden whiteness around his mouth. Eagerly, she grasped at the chance to redeem herself.

'Here,' she said quickly, 'let me get those for you.'

But he had already snatched the crutches and was rising to his feet. 'You wouldn't have taken my calls if you'd been watching your spider plants grow.' He grunted as he jammed the crutches under his arms, and his eyes met hers. 'I want to know why.'

Gabrielle ran her tongue across her lips. 'This really isn't the place to talk about it, James. I...'

'Mr Forrester?'

They both looked at the nurse striding briskly towards them. James's expression changed and he smiled.

'Ah,' he said lightly, 'my angel of mercy.'

'Your gaoler, if you don't watch out,' the nurse said sternly, and she turned towards Gabrielle. 'Miss Shelton?' Gabrielle nodded and she pressed a sheaf of papers into her hands. 'Instructions,' she said. 'How to apply compresses to Mr Forrester's knee and jaw. And a prescription to fill, if aspirin isn't enough to ease any discomfort.'

Gabrielle looked at her helplessly. 'But I'm not——'

'See to it he gets enough fluids. And he needs a proper diet. He's to keep off that leg, doctor says. No weight on it at all until the swelling goes down. Have you a cane at home?'

'A cane?' Gabrielle repeated in bewilderment.

'Well, no matter. You can purchase one at the surgical pharmacy when he's ready to trade in the crutches for something lighter. Doctor says we'll see him again in ten days to remove the sutures.'

'I'm afraid there's been some mistake. I'm not——'

'You're going to frighten Miss Shelton off with all those directives,' James said smoothly. 'I promise she's not going to have any difficulty with me. I'll behave.'

The nurse nodded. 'You'd better, or you'll end up in the orthopaedics ward, where you probably should be right now.'

James smiled charmingly. 'Not to worry,' he said. 'I'll be good.'

A smile twitched at the corners of the nurse's mouth, then vanished. 'I doubt that,' she said, and then she turned and hurried back towards the examining-rooms.

Gabrielle turned slowly towards James. 'What on earth did you tell them?' she asked warily.

'Only what I had to so I could get myself out of here,' he muttered. 'Don't look so panicked, Gabrielle. Your responsibility to me ends at the gate. Just look solicitous, walk me out of the door, and that will be the end of it.' He shifted the crutches beneath his arms, then glanced at her. 'You can manage that, can't you?'

'But—but shouldn't you stay in the hospital? Your knee...' She watched incredulously as he began hobbling off and then she hurried after him.

'I told you, the knee's an old injury. I know how to care for it.'

Gabrielle sprang past him and pushed open the swinging doors. 'Did you tell them I'd take care of you? James—you did, didn't you?'

He sighed. 'I told you, I didn't ask them to call you. But once they said they had ... Look, I'd have promised them the moon to get out of here. But you don't have to worry about it—it's not as if anyone's going to check.'

'But you heard what the nurse said. You need rest. And care. Medication. You can't get all that in a hotel.'

She fell silent as James looked at her. For a moment, she thought she'd seen something flare to life in his eyes, something that was triumphant and almost frightening in its intensity. But then he turned away, and, when he looked at her again, whatever she'd imagined was gone.

'I'll manage, Gabrielle. Just play along until we're out of here.'

The rain had lessened to a drizzle. As they stepped out of the door, tendrils of fog curled around them. Gabrielle shivered and pulled up her coat-collar. 'There's a bench over there,' she said. 'Why don't you sit down while I get my car?'

James shook his head. 'You don't have to bother. I'll walk out to the street and find a taxi.'

He began moving across the circular drive that fronted the hospital, his crutches swinging steadily. Drops of water caught in his dark hair, glistening there like tiny jewels.

Gabrielle watched him go and then she hurried after him. 'Don't be silly, James. I'll drive you to your hotel.'

'I told you, you don't have to bother. I'll be fine.'

'It's no bother. We're almost to my car—it's that blue Toyota, over there.'

The rhythmic swing of the crutches stopped and James looked at her. 'You spent the day avoiding me,' he said flatly. 'The last thing I want to do is force myself on you now.'

Colour pinkened her cheeks. 'You're not,' she said quickly. 'And I didn't try to avoid you today.'

His eyes met hers. 'Didn't you?'

They were back to that, and she still had no answer. At least, she had none she wanted him to hear. Guilt stirred within her again. Maybe she hadn't been driving his car, but wasn't she at least partly responsible for his accident?

'James,' her voice was low but steady, 'I'd really like to help you. Please, let me take you to your hotel and help you settle in.'

Again, she thought she saw that flash of something in his eyes before he turned away from her.

'You said you were very busy.'

'Alma can handle things.' She put her hand on his arm. 'Please. I'd like to do it.'

When he looked at her this time, he gave her the same boyish grin he'd offered the nurse.

'All right. Thank you, Gabrielle. I'd be very grateful.'

She winced as she watched him settle into her little car and carefully stretch his injured leg as much as the cramped space allowed. She drove more slowly than usual, avoiding the more obvious bumps in the road, holding her breath each time she caused an inadvertent lurch.

Not that James complained. She thought he was asleep, at first; he'd put the seat back as far as it would go, and he sat with his head resting against the cushion, his eyes closed.

But he was awake. When she accelerated at a traffic light, he opened his eyes and looked at her.

'Better watch that,' he said with a little laugh. 'That's how I did myself in.'

'I didn't want to disturb you—you were sleeping.'

He went on staring at her for a moment, and then he turned his head and looked out of the windscreen. 'It's too late for that, Gabrielle.'

Her heart turned over. 'What do you mean?'

'Why wouldn't you take my calls today?'

Her mouth went dry. 'Must you keep asking me that?'

'I spent half last night thinking about you,' he said.

And I spent half last night thinking about you, too, she thought. But it wasn't the same. 'We had a nice evening,' she said stiffly, her eyes on the road. 'But...'

'But you'd decided you weren't going to see me again.'

Startled, she looked over at him. He was watching her narrowly, his face dark and unreadable.

'Yes,' she said after a pause. 'That's right, I did.'

James shifted in the seat. 'Can you tell me why?'

She swallowed drily. 'I—I can't, no. It's too complicated.'

His hand closed over hers. 'Is it because you don't trust me?'

A pulse beat in her throat. 'Why do you say that?' she whispered.

He sighed and leaned his head back. 'The day I came to your shop, you were full of questions about the way we'd met and the things I knew about you.'

Her laughter was forced. 'I was, yes. But you can't blame me for that. Alma says it's because I'm from the north.'

He smiled. 'She's right. New Yorkers are the most suspicious lot in the world.'

Gabrielle's smile vanished. 'I didn't say I was a New Yorker, James. How did you——?'

'Didn't you?'

'No.' Her voice was sharp.

He shrugged his shoulders. 'I'm sure you did.'

'I didn't. I never——'

'But you are from there, aren't you?' She nodded, reluctantly, and he laughed easily. 'Well, then, it was a lucky guess. I went to university in the city; I can still tell a New York accent without half trying.'

Gabrielle drew a deep breath, then let it out. What he'd said made sense. On one of her college courses, the teacher had been able to determine where the students were from by the way they spoke.

'But I don't blame you for not being ready to trust just anybody, Gabrielle. It's a mistake not to question motives. You'd be a fool not to have learned that by now.'

This time, his words sent a chill dancing along her spine. 'What do you mean?'

His hand tightened on hers until she feared her bones would be crushed, and then the pressure eased. When he spoke, his tone was light and teasing.

'I'd have thought beautiful women learned to distrust half the men in the world by the time they passed puberty. But you can trust me, of course.'

She looked at him. 'Can I?'

He flashed her a quick smile. 'How could anyone not trust a man with his trousers sliced open?'

His eyes were warm, his expression open, and finally Gabrielle smiled too.

'How, indeed?' she said.

James grinned. 'I'll remedy that as soon as we reach my hotel. Turn right at the next corner.'

Maison Lillian was a small, elegant building several blocks from La Vie en Rose. Delicate wrought-iron balconies graced its upper storeys, and Gabrielle could im-

agine the way the hotel would look when the weather
warmed and sultry greenery hung from the balconies and
trellised walls.

She pulled in before the hotel, ignoring the 'no
parking' sign, then hurried around to the passenger side
of the car so she could help James on to the pavement.

'If you don't behave, I'll take you back to the hospital
and hand you over to the nurse,' she said when he pro-
tested. She hovered beside him as he edged his way up
the narrow steps that led to the lobby. 'Can you manage?'

He nodded. 'No problem.'

But she saw the beads of sweat on his forehead, and
she was glad when they topped the final step and entered
the hotel. James moved slowly towards the reception
desk. The concierge looked up, her face crumpling with
concern when she saw him.

'Mr Forrester! What happened?'

James smiled reassuringly. 'Just a little accident,
madame. If I could have my key?'

She nodded. 'Of course,' she said, taking a key from
the board behind her. Her forehead creased in thought
as she handed it over. 'You'll never manage the stairs,
Mr Forrester. Not like that.'

James frowned. 'You're right, of course. How foolish
of me.'

Gabrielle looked from him to the concierge. 'Isn't there
an elevator?'

He shook his head. 'Not since yesterday. It's an old
one...'

'An antique, Mr Forrester,' the concierge said quickly.

James smiled, but Gabrielle thought she could see the
exhaustion that underlay it.

'As *madame* says, the elevator's an antique. It's going
to take some time to get the proper parts to repair it.'

The woman nodded again. 'Exactly.'

'A different room, then, *madame*? Something on this
level?'

The concierge frowned. 'I'm terribly sorry, Mr Forrester, but it's almost Carnival. We have no rooms.'

'The next floor, then. I can manage——'

'We have no rooms,' the woman repeated. 'None at all.'

Gabrielle put her hand on James's shoulder. 'That's all right,' she said quickly. 'We'll find you a room elsewhere.'

Madame's thin brows rose delicately. 'Are you from New Orleans, *mademoiselle*?'

'No. Well, yes, yes, I am, but I'm new——'

'You are indeed, or you would know there are no rooms available only days before *mardi gras*.' She dismissed Gabrielle with a wave of her hand. 'I shall have the bellman pack your luggage and bring it down while I make enquiries for you, Mr Forrester, but where you'll be able to find a suitable room in New Orleans now is anybody's guess.'

Hours later, the woman's patronising words had proven all too true. Gabrielle had driven through the streets of the Quarter, then through the Garden District and the Downtown area, but the story was the same at each hotel.

All rooms had been booked weeks and months in advance. The doorman at one of the larger hotels had taken pity on them; he'd given them the name of a woman who took in boarders. She had no rooms, either, but she gave Gabrielle a list of rooming houses that took her in all directions, only to hear the same message.

James had waited in the car. 'I'll come with you,' he'd insisted the first few times, but finally he'd simply nodded when Gabrielle said it was foolish for them both to make enquiries. 'All right,' he'd said, and his quick acquiescence, coupled with the drawn expression on his face, caught at Gabrielle's heart.

'Are you in pain, James?' she'd asked softly.

'No, of course not,' he'd said. But it had needed no crystal ball to know he was lying.

By nightfall, the Toyota was parked outside a dilapidated old house in one of New Orleans' less desirable neighbourhoods. Gabrielle sighed as she opened the door and got into the car.

'Don't tell me,' James said. 'There's no room at the inn.'

Gabrielle looked at him. His tone was light, but she knew it masked his exhaustion. She could see his face clearly in the pool of light from a street lamp. He looked worn and vulnerable, and her heart went out to him.

Where next? she thought. She'd run through the list the doorman had given her. There was no place left to try. If only she knew someone with a spare room.

Her pulse quickened. No, she couldn't do that. It was impossible...

'Look,' he said tiredly, 'you've done more than enough. Why not drive me back to Maison Lillian and I'll throw myself on *madame's* mercy? There's a couch in the lobby.'

'The one in the corner?' Gabrielle shook her head. 'It was a love-seat, James. You'd never get any rest.'

He grimaced and rubbed his knee. 'The hospital, then. It's probably the only place in town with an available room. I suppose I can survive one night in Orthopaedics.'

Gabrielle swallowed drily. 'There's—there's another place.'

James grunted and shifted his leg. 'Damn! I should have taken those tablets Nurse Ramrod was pushing.'

'Does your knee hurt?'

He didn't answer, but one look at him told her it had been a foolish question. His face was pale, his eyes closed, the lashes dark against his cheeks. Gabrielle bit down on her lip, and then she started the engine and pulled away from the kerb.

'Where to?' James murmured. He sighed and looked at her. 'If the next place looks like the last, I'd just as soon pass.'

She smiled. 'I guarantee it's much nicer, and I know for a fact there's a room.'

'The woman's hallucinating,' he said with a groan. 'Have you been hitting Nurse Ramrod's pills?'

Gabrielle laughed. 'I'm perfectly sober, James.' She slowed the car as they approached a red light and smiled at him. 'Remember the other night when you dined *chez Gabrielle*?'

James sighed. 'The woman's not only sober, she's starved. Forgive me—I forgot all about dinner. Look, why don't you stop somewhere and let me buy us a meal? Then you can drive me back to—to...'

'To where? We've tried every place in the city.'

He shrugged. 'I told you. To my hotel. Or to the hospital. Don't worry about me—I'll think of something.'

'I already have.' She drew a deep breath as the light changed and she eased the car forward. 'I don't have any steaks in the freezer, but I do have eggs and bacon.'

'I told you, you've done more than enough. I'm not going to let you make dinner, too.'

Gabrielle lifted her chin. 'You're not only dining *chez Gabrielle*, you're going to stay there.'

James stared at her. 'What are you talking about?'

'Look, there's not a hotel room within a hundred miles of New Orleans. I have an extra bedroom, right on the main level, and there's a WC and a shower just off the kitchen.'

He shook his head. 'No, I couldn't impose. I——'

'You wouldn't be imposing. I—I've been uncomfortable lately; the carriage house is old, you know, and at night it squeaks and moans and...' She cleared her throat. 'You'd be doing me a favour, when you come down to it.'

'That's quite an about-face,' he said slowly. 'First you spend the day avoiding me, and now you invite me to move in with you.' A slow grin creased the corners of his eyes. 'Not that I'd mind, of course, if that's what you want.'

Gabrielle hesitated. Was it what she wanted? Only hours ago, she'd had a list of good reasons for never seeing James Forrester again, and now she was offering to share her home with him.

'Yes,' she said quickly. 'Yes, I'm sure. It's—it's what I want.'

James laughed softly. 'Well, then, how can I possibly refuse?'

There was something in his laugh, in the silky tone of his voice, that made her breath catch. She looked across the car at him. Was it the light, or had some of the weariness fled his face? He moved in the seat, and for a second it seemed that even his leg was more mobile.

Gabrielle looked away from him. No. That was impossible. He'd been in an automobile accident. There was no way you could exaggerate that. And she was doing the only decent thing. She was giving him a room. It was the least she could do for a man who'd done so much for her.

It was nothing but a humanitarian gesture. And it was harmless—wasn't it?

She felt her pulse begin to beat in her temple, like the throb of a distant drum. Was it apprehension or was it excitement? she wondered.

He reached across the console and covered her hand with his, and the change in tempo of her heart was all the answer she needed.

CHAPTER SIX

'I HOPE you don't mind sharing quarters with all these boxes,' Gabrielle said as she switched on the light in the little room down the hall from the kitchen. 'I never did get around to unpacking everything after I moved in.'

James leaned his crutches against a maple dresser, then hopped to the narrow brass bed tucked against the wall and sank down on it.

'The room's fine,' he said with a tired smile. 'Tonight, I don't think I'd mind sharing quarters with a Marine battalion.'

Gabrielle smiled as she opened the wardrobe. 'The worst you might have to put up with are one or two mice,' she said, tugging blankets and pillows from the shelf. 'The house must have been empty quite a while before I moved in. I've gotten rid of just about all of them, but every once in a while a straggler turns up.'

'Just as long as they don't snore, I won't say a word.'

'Now,' she said, dropping the linens on the foot of the bed, 'what would you like for supper? Soup? Crackers...' Her questions trailed off as she looked at James. He was sitting with his head back against the wall, his eyes closed. In the unyielding light of the ceiling fixture, his exhaustion was easy to see, and she wondered how she'd ever, even for a moment, doubted it. 'James?' she said softly. 'Are you all right?'

He opened his eyes and nodded. 'Fine. I'm just a little tired.' He winced as he straightened his leg. 'All I need is some rest and I'll be good as new.'

'Won't you let me fill the prescription the hospital gave you?'

'No,' he said, sitting forward and gently rubbing his bandaged knee. 'There's no need. I told you, I've gone this route before.'

'Yes, but it would ease the pain.'

'The prescription's for a narcotic.' His voice was suddenly sharp. 'Something that dulls your reflexes and puts you to sleep.'

Gabrielle smiled a little. 'And what a terrible thing that would be if someone's hurting,' she said gently.

James's eyes met hers. 'Chalk it off to male ego,' he said after a pause. 'OK?'

Her smile broadened. 'How about food? Does this ego of yours extend to that, too, or shall I make you something to eat?'

He grinned. 'I was hoping you'd ask.'

'What would you like? Soup? Bacon and eggs? Toast? Jam?'

James laughed. 'All of that, and a gallon of coffee besides.'

'And two aspirin. Don't say "no",' she warned when he began to shake his head. 'If you do, I'll take you back to St Francis and turn you over to Nurse Ramrod.'

'I surrender,' he said, laughing as he held up his hands. 'You wouldn't believe the terrible things that woman threatened me with today. I had to promise her you were a cross between Florence Nightingale and the Good Fairy.'

Gabrielle looked at him. 'You played a risky game, didn't you? I mean, you weren't even sure I'd come.'

'Once they said they'd called you, I never doubted you would.'

His gaze moved over her face, intimate as a caress. Gabrielle's pulse leaped in unexpected response, and she turned away from him.

'Soup will be on in ten minutes,' she said, and before he could answer she stepped out of the room and closed the door behind her.

She leaned against it and drew a deep breath. She felt drained—all her energies had gone into the past few minutes, into smiling and talking with a casual indifference, as if the realisation that she'd really brought James to stay with her hadn't sent a sudden shock through all her senses.

Not that she hadn't known what she was doing when she'd asked him to stay at the carriage house—it was just that the reality had been different from how she'd imagined it. It had been almost overpowering: stepping into the dark foyer with James behind her had been like walking into another dimension, one in which there was no sound louder than her own suddenly erratic heartbeat.

James had felt it, too. She knew it, even though he hadn't spoken. She'd heard it in his quickly indrawn breath, felt it in the tension instantly flowing between them with the potency of a force field.

She'd pushed by him and hurried through the main level of the carriage house, throwing on all the lights, chattering brightly about the spare room, apologising for its condition, and all the time she'd been almost painfully aware of James's nearness and the way he seemed to fill the little house with his presence.

Now, as she switched on the kitchen light, she felt almost light-headed. Well, why wouldn't she? She hadn't eaten anything in hours. And James wasn't the only one who needed aspirin: her head felt as if someone had tied a tourniquet around it.

She got down the bottle of aspirin, shook two tablets into her hand, and gulped them down with a swallow of water. Two more for James—no, three, and she wouldn't brook any arguments. He had this ridiculous male thing about taking medicines—her father had been the same, until the pain got too strong—but he'd either take the three tablets or she'd force them down his throat.

Gabrielle laughed softly as she opened the fridge door and peered inside. That was a thought, wasn't it? James was all lean muscle; she'd be helpless against him. His strength had frightened her when he'd come barging through the door last night.

Last night. How could that be? How could things have turned upside-down so fast? This morning, she'd vowed never to see him again, and now, instead of fearing him, she—she what?

Stop that. Concentrate on making supper. That's it. That's the way.

Her hands shook as she took a loaf of bread from the fridge. There were only a few slices, barely enough for two. The egg carton was almost empty—well, James could have the three that were left. At least there was half a pound of bacon. She made a face as she carefully plucked away the discoloured top slice and tossed it into the dustbin.

The cupboard was no more promising. A couple of tins of soup, a half-box of crackers—stale, probably. At least there was coffee and sugar, although if James liked cream with his coffee he was out of luck.

She filled the kettle, then set out the Chemex. In the morning, early, she could pop out to that little shop around the corner, the one with all the delicious smells drifting out of the door. They baked their own breads and sweet rolls—what was it James had said he wanted? *Beignets*, that was it. She'd buy fresh-made *beignets* and a pound of New Orleans coffee, aromatic with chicory, and when he awoke he'd find breakfast waiting.

For dinner—she smiled as she whipped the eggs and added a splash of cold water in lieu of milk—dinner could be a little more exotic. There was that old cookbook she'd found in the cupboard, the one with all those Creole and Cajun specialities in it—things like shrimp jambalaya and crawfish gumbo. She could get all the ingredients at the farmers market, where the air was redolent of spices and court bouillon. And the next

day, if he felt up to it, they could drive out to one of
the plantations Alma had told her about and . . .

Gabrielle stopped in the centre of the room. What was
she doing? She was trembling with excitement, planning
for tomorrow and the next day with a man she knew
nothing about. What had happened to all her questions?
What had become of caution?

'Ah, that coffee smells wonderful.'

Her heart turned over and she whirled towards the
doorway, her hand pressed to her breast. 'I didn't hear
you,' she said with a nervous laugh.

James had managed to change his torn trousers and
soiled shirt. But the repairs only emphasised the toll the
accident had taken. His face was drawn with fatigue, the
skin a mask beneath which the bones showed in harsh
relief. Shadows lay dark beneath his eyes; the bruise on
his jaw had turned as black as the tiny silk stitches that
angled across his cheek.

Gabrielle hurried to the table and pulled out a chair.
'Sit down, James,' she said. 'You look exhausted.'

He nodded as he crossed the room, the rubber-tipped
crutches squeaking against the tiled floor.

'To tell the truth, I feel pretty rocky.' He eased the
crutches from beneath his arms and sank into a chair.
'But a cup of that coffee will fix me up in no time.'

'Aspirin first,' she said, holding out her hand. James
looked at the three tablets and then at Gabrielle, whose
eyebrows rose dramatically. 'You don't get coffee unless
you down those first.'

He grinned. 'Nurse Ramrod would be proud of you.'
The aspirin went down with a swallow of water. 'Satisfied, Doctor?'

Gabrielle smiled. 'Yes. For that, you not only get
coffee, you get soup. And crackers,' she added, setting
a plate of them down before him, 'although I'm afraid
they're pretty stale.'

He bit into a cracker and smiled. 'They taste like ambrosia. And for God's sake, don't apologise. It's not as if you expected a house guest, is it?'

'I'm just sorry I kept you riding around in my little car for so many hours. I should have known we'd never find a room anywhere, not with *mardi gras* only days away.'

He inhaled deeply as she served the soup. 'Mmm, that smells wonderful. What is it?'

She laughed as she slipped into the seat opposite him. 'Campbell's Chicken Gumbo, straight from the tin. I figured that, now that I was a southerner, I ought to make some concessions to local custom.'

James spooned up some soup and swallowed it. 'It must take some doing,' he said, 'making the adjustment from being a New Yorker to being a—what do they say, an Orleanian?'

Gabrielle smiled. 'Alma's trying to help me manage. I don't think she's very satisfied with my progress, though.'

He grinned at her. 'This morning, when I called the shop, I asked her what it would take to get you to the phone, and she sighed and said she'd didn't know, that you were a damn Yankee and sometimes you just didn't have the sense God gave mules.'

She laughed softly. 'If she weren't so nice, and I didn't need her so badly, I think I'd resent that.'

James swallowed another mouthful of soup. 'She says that you keep to yourself too much.'

Gabrielle's back stiffened. 'I love Alma dearly,' she said, 'but she talks too much.' She pushed back her chair, collected the empty soup bowls, and carried them to the sink.

'Hey,' his voice was soft, 'she meant well. The lady's very fond of you.'

Some of the tension eased from her shoulders. 'I know she is,' she said finally. 'It's just that she—she has a different view of life. She has this—this southern attitude, a kind of trusting way of dealing with people and things.'

'And you don't.'

It was a statement, not a question. Gabrielle shook her head. 'No, I don't. I've had to learn the hard way that things aren't always what they seem...' Her voice faded and died. 'Besides, Alma doesn't really know anything about me.'

James watched her as she placed a platter of bacon and eggs before him. 'I'm not sure I do either,' he said after a moment.

Her eyes met his. 'Aren't you? You seem to know a lot, James,' she said, watching him. 'The things I like to eat and drink, where I'm from...'

His face gave nothing away. 'Good guesses, that's all. But I'm not sure I know the real you.'

Her pulse tripped. 'The real me?'

James nodded. His pale eyes held hers. 'Yes. I realised last night, I know very little about Gabrielle Shelton.'

'There's not much to know. My father died a few months ago and I decided to start my life over. So I came here, to New Orleans...'

'You make it sound simple.'

The tone of his voice made her head come up. He was watching her narrowly, a smile on his face, but the smile looked as if it had been pasted on.

'What do you mean?'

James shrugged. 'It must be hard to leave everyone you care about.'

She shook her head. 'I told you, my father died. He was all I had.'

James's eyes were fixed on hers. 'Surely there was someone else?'

'No. No one.'

'No one?' His voice was soft, almost a whisper. 'No one at all?'

She thought of Tony Vitale—Uncle Tony—and she hesitated. 'There was—there was someone,' she said finally. 'But it wasn't—it didn't . . .'

'A man.' His voice was flat.

Their eyes met. His expression was dark and unreadable; she had the sudden feeling that he knew she carried a burden within her, a secret that had become too heavy to bear. Suddenly, crazily, the desire to tell him the truth almost overwhelmed her.

She looked down at the table. Bacon fat had congealed on her plate; the sight of it made her feel nauseated and her stomach rose involuntarily. Finally she nodded her head.

'Yes.' The admission made her dizzy. 'A man. My . . .' she hesitated, then swallowed hard. 'My uncle.'

James leaned across the table. 'Tell me about him, Gabrielle.'

She looked up at him. She was tired of carrying her old identity hidden inside herself. And yet, how could she unburden herself to a stranger? Even if she did, where would she begin? There was her father's illness and the trial she'd walked away from; there was the man she called 'Uncle' whom others called a criminal; there were the cruel lies the tabloids had woven about her.

'Did you leave New York because of him?'

She shook her head. 'No. Not exactly.'

'Not exactly.' James's voice was soft. 'What does that mean?'

Gabrielle ran her tongue across her lips. 'I can't—I can't explain. I told you, it's complicated.'

James drew a deep breath. 'This uncle of yours—did you love him?'

The question seemed a strange one to ask. His voice was dispassionate, almost removed. Gabrielle lifted her eyes to his; her breath caught at the fierce sharpness of his stare.

'No,' she said, surprise triggering her unplanned response. 'I didn't.' An overpowering memory of the way Vitale had taken to touching her made her shiver. 'I thought I did once, but...'

'But?' James's tone was edged.

Gabrielle drew a shuddering breath. 'It isn't easy to explain,' she said softly. 'He was very good to me, James. He—he gave me everything. He paid for everything...'

She fell silent. James must think she was crazy. He was watching her with such a strange look on his face, his eyes narrowed until she could only see the palest glint of blue behind his dark lashes. Half of what she'd said made no sense, and half sounded like a bad soap opera, murky and heavy with tragedy.

She felt as if she'd been teetering on the edge of a precipice. She'd come far too close to saying things she shouldn't. It was impossible to tell this story to anyone without its sounding like a hackneyed catastrophe. That was one of the reasons she'd decided never to talk about that part of her life again. The other reason was even more important. She had had enough of raised eyebrows and sly looks when people learned she was Gabrielle Chiari.

She knew beyond certainty that the only way to forget the past was to bury it.

'I told you,' she said finally, 'it's hard to explain.' Their eyes met and Gabrielle managed a quick smile. 'Let's talk about something else. Tell me about yourself. I don't know a thing about you, James. I——'

His hand closed over hers. 'Have you finished with this man or is he still in your life?'

'James, please. I told you——'

'Just answer the question.' His fingers tightened on hers. 'How do you feel about him now?'

She sighed deeply. It was as if his eyes were drawing the answers to his questions from her.

'I don't know. Sometimes I think—sometimes I think I'm done with him. But then I remember—I remember the way it was, the way it used to be...'

'You mean, you remember the things he used to give you. The gifts.'

She looked at him, surprise etched into her face. 'No, I didn't mean——'

'This is an expensive house. Did you buy it with his money?'

His voice was as hard as forged steel and just as cold. Her head came up sharply and she looked at him, cheeks flushed. 'My father's insurance policy was the down payment. And I don't think I like the way you said that, James.'

His lips drew back from his teeth. 'I was only repeating your words, Gabrielle. You said he gave you things.'

'Yes. But you—you gave it a different meaning. He was my uncle, but you made it sound...' Her breath caught; suddenly, all her suspicions about him were reawakened. 'Who are you?' she whispered, pulling her hand from his. 'What do you want from me?'

He stared at her while the kitchen clock ticked away the seconds, and then a crooked smile twisted across his face.

'I wish to hell I knew,' he said.

'I—I don't understand.'

'Gabrielle.' His hand tightened on hers and he leaned towards her. 'Let me help you. You can't run forever.'

Her face paled. 'What do you mean?'

'I'm not a fool, Gabrielle. Let me help you. I know you're running from something.'

'I'm not,' she said quickly. 'I told you, my father's death was hard for me.' She pulled her hand from his;

her chair squeaked as she pushed it back and got to her feet. 'It only hurts to talk about the past.'

'You can't ignore the past, dammit!' James's tone was harsh. 'You have to make peace with it. If you don't, sooner or later it'll catch up with you.'

'Don't say that!' Gabrielle turned away and wrapped her arms around herself. 'If I let myself believe that, I'd never be able to face tomorrow. The past is over,' she said in a voice that trembled. 'It has to be.'

She heard the rasp of James's chair as he shoved back from the table, then the drag of a crutch as he moved towards her.

'It can't be over if you're still running from it.'

'I told you, I'm not. You don't even know what I'm talking about, James. You——'

'Gabrielle. Face whatever you're afraid of. Face it squarely and then you can put it behind you.' He put his free hand on her shoulder and clasped her tightly. 'If you don't, you'll never be able to get on with your life.'

She shook her head. 'You don't understand,' she whispered.

James drew in his breath. 'I want to,' he said softly. 'Tell me what you're afraid of, Gabrielle. Trust me. Let me help you.'

She felt herself tremble beneath his touch. She thought of last night and how he'd held her and comforted her, how he'd kissed away her tears—and how she'd spent the night wondering what it was he wanted from her.

'Trust me,' he'd said.

She did. Didn't she? Hadn't she made peace with her fears? She must have; she'd taken James Forrester into her home, hadn't she? Surely that meant something?

She turned towards him. Maybe it was the time to believe in someone. Maybe that someone was James. Maybe...

Gabrielle's hand flew to her mouth. How could she have been so selfish? Caught up in her own misery, she'd all but forgotten how ill he was. The aspirin hadn't done any good at all: his colour was ashen, his eyes dark slits in his taut face. Her eyes moved over the gash on his cheek, where the stitches rose darkly against the swollen and reddened skin.

'James,' she said, 'you look terrible.'

His expression remained implacable. Then, slowly, a smile curved over his mouth. 'Flattery will get you nowhere,' he said. 'But that's one hell of a way to change the subject.'

'Here, lean on me and let me get you back to the chair.' She put her arm around his waist and led him to the table. 'There. Sit down. That's it. Do you want to put your leg on this footstool? I should have thought of it before; I——'

He caught her hand as she knelt beside him. 'Gabrielle. Tell me what you were going to say a minute ago.'

'I wasn't going to say anything.'

'You were. I know you were.'

She shook her head. 'It wasn't important. Anyway, it's something I have to work out alone.'

James brought her hand to his lips. 'You're not alone,' he said softly. 'Not any more.'

Inexplicably, tears rose in her eyes. She blinked them back, but not before dampness welled on her lashes.

'James,' she whispered, 'James...'

He drew her to him, one arm curving about her. 'Gabrielle,' he said thickly, 'don't cry.'

'Your knee. James, you'll hurt yourself.'

His eyes darkened. 'It's you I'm afraid of hurting,' he muttered. 'You, Gabrielle. You...'

He pulled her into the hardness of his body and his mouth fell on hers like a stone, taking hers with a hot, open abandon that sent the blood pulsing wildly through her veins. His lips parted hers quickly, hungrily, as if he were dying of thirst for her.

Gabrielle moaned as his tongue thrust between her lips. The sweet taste of him filled her mouth; her head fell back and her hands rose between them, moving against his chest. Her fingers twisted in his shirt, then flattened against him. The strong, swift beat of his heart pounded beneath her palms.

James groaned against her mouth and drew her closer. His hand moved along the flare of her hip and to her buttocks, cupping the curve and bringing her tightly against him. She felt his body stir and quicken against hers, the hard power of his erection more erotic than anything she'd ever imagined. She moved against him in unconscious need and he groaned again.

'Yes,' he said, 'do that. Do that...'

His mouth fell to her throat, his kisses hot, his teeth sharp as he followed the long, curving arch. He whispered her name as he cupped the back of her head and brought her face to his, whispered it again as he kissed her.

Gabrielle was dazed with desire; she was aware of her body in ways she'd never been before. Everywhere James touched her, tendrils of flame seemed to ignite beneath her skin. Her blood felt thick and sluggish. There was a strange sensation low in her belly, as if something were spreading its wings within her.

She moaned as James ran his hand along her back and traced the outline of her ribs through her thin cotton sweater, moaned again when his fingertips grazed the underswell of her breast. When finally he cupped her breast, she cried out and James bent to her, caught her cry in his mouth, returned it to her as a groan of his own impassioned need. She shuddered as she felt the fierce hardening of her nipple in his seeking hand.

James whispered something to her, her name, perhaps something more intimate—she was beyond the ability to understand anything but her desperate need to be close to him. Still kneeling between his legs, she pressed herself to him so that her breasts flattened against his chest while he feasted on the sweetness of her mouth.

'James,' she whispered, her voice soft and urgent. 'James...'

Her hands lifted and she caught his face between her palms. His unshaved skin rasped against her flesh; it sent a savage passion spiralling deep within her, and she thought of how that roughened skin would feel against the softness of her breasts or the tender, secret flesh between her thighs.

Her body fell limp against his and he caught her to him, moulding the length of her to him while he kissed her. She moaned softly; her hands cupped his face more tightly while she raised herself to him, offered herself to him.

His breath hissed sharply. 'Gabrielle,' he whispered, and he caught her hand and lifted it from his sutured cheek.

Her eyes opened and focused on his face. The realisation that she'd touched his wound came slowly; when finally it did, she recoiled in horror.

'James,' she whispered. 'Oh, I'm sorry.'

His smile was quick and taut. 'It wasn't your fault, love. Don't apologise.'

'Have I hurt you?'

He shook his head. 'I'm fine.'

She knew he was telling her what he wanted her to hear. But his eyes told another story, as did the play of muscle beside his mouth.

Gabrielle took her hand from his and lay it against his chest. His heart was still racing, as was hers.

'I—I wasn't thinking, James. I...'

James cupped her face and lifted it to his. 'I'd have been insulted if you had.'

Gabrielle smiled. 'Just imagine what Nurse Ramrod would do if she found out.'

'Throttle you,' he said solemnly. 'And banish me to the orthopaedics floor.' His eyes were warm on hers and his thumbs moved lightly over her cheeks. 'A fate worse than death.'

'I tell you what,' she said teasingly, 'I won't tell anyone if you don't.'

'Cross your heart?'

She laughed. 'Your terrible secret is safe with me.' She caught her breath as James's smile faltered and his face grew dark. She thought she'd never seen such pain in a man's eyes before. 'James? I *did* hurt you, didn't I?'

He bent to her and kissed her with a fierceness that stole her breath away, and then his mouth gentled on hers. When he raised his head, the darkness had left his eyes. He smiled and cupped her chin gently in his palm.

'You've taken good care of me. Nurse Ramrod would be pleased.'

Gabrielle smiled back. 'No, she wouldn't. You should have been asleep hours ago.'

He sighed. 'You're probably right. It has been one hell of a long day, hasn't it?' He traced the outline of her mouth with his thumb, and then he let her go and rose slowly to his feet. 'Goodnight,' he said. 'Sleep well.'

'I will,' she said without thinking, 'knowing you're here.' His eyes met hers and she gave a little laugh. 'I—I haven't been sleeping so well lately. I know it's silly...'

James's mouth turned down at the edges. 'There's nothing silly about it,' he said, and then he drew a breath. 'But there's nothing to worry about tonight, Gabrielle. I promise you that.'

She watched as he set his crutches in place and started down the hall. How strange, she thought. A little while ago, James's sudden appearance in her life had disturbed her. Now, his presence made her feel more secure than she had in months.

She took a step forward and murmured his name. When he paused and looked back at her, she smiled. 'Sleep well,' she said.

Darkness, like a giant fist, closed over his face again. For a heartbeat, Gabrielle felt as if she was looking into the eyes of a stranger.

'Goodnight,' he said finally.

The door to the spare room opened, then closed after him, and she was alone.

CHAPTER SEVEN

THE early morning streets of the French Quarter were drenched in sunlight. Puddles of rainwater, remnants of yesterday's storm, gleamed along the pavement. Gutters and roofs still dripped gently in those shady corners where the sun had yet to reach. But the sky was a cloudless blue and the breeze warm. It was as if an early spring had settled over the city.

By the time Gabrielle finished her morning run to the flower shop, her shorts and cotton T-shirt were dark with perspiration. She'd half expected some sly comment from Alma. But her assistant was too distressed by the details of James's accident to take anything but casual notice of Gabrielle's unladylike appearance.

'That poor man,' she said, taking a towel from the shelf in the back room and tossing it to Gabrielle, 'hurtin' his knee and all. I'm just glad he's all right. I kept hopin' you'd call and let me know how he was.'

'I meant to.' Gabrielle blotted her face and neck, then draped the towel around her shoulders. 'But—well, things got kind of hectic.' She hesitated. 'We had to find James a new place to stay. The elevator at his hotel was out of order, and he couldn't manage the stairs.'

'However did you find anythin'?' Alma asked in amazement. 'There's never a room left by the time *mardi gras* weekend rolls around.'

Gabrielle looked at her. Now was the time to tell her that she'd taken James to her house. But the words caught in her throat. The memory of James as she'd seen him when she peeped into his room this morning, asleep and sprawled across the narrow bed with the blanket tangled at his hips, was still too vivid.

She shrugged her shoulders. 'We finally worked something out.'

'I can't imagine how—unless he found a room in some dilapidated hole in the wall across the river. How's he goin' to enjoy Carnival if——'

Gabrielle tossed the towel aside. 'Speaking of Carnival,' she said quickly, 'didn't you say the Hyacinth Club is going to parade this afternoon?'

Alma rolled her eyes. 'Folks call them "krewes", Gaby, not "clubs". And it's the Irises, not the Hyacinths, for goodness' sake.'

Gabrielle grinned. 'Well, I was close.'

The older woman laughed. 'Sure. You got the parade date right. Which reminds me—if you want to get close enough to see anythin', we should get to Rampart Street early. I thought we might...'

Gabrielle glanced at her watch as Alma spoke, her voice bubbling with excitement. She'd been gone more than half an hour; was James still asleep? she wondered. She'd left a note in the kitchen, tucked beneath a carafe of orange juice, but she wanted to be there when he awakened. It would be nice to have a breakfast of fresh coffee and warm *beignets* on the terrace. The sun and the soft morning air might be the best kind of medicine.

'So what do you think, Gaby? Shall we?'

Gabrielle blinked. Her assistant was looking at her, eyebrows raised.

'I'm sorry, Alma, I guess I was daydreaming. I didn't hear you.'

Alma sighed. 'I was saying' there won't be any business to speak of today. We only have two bouquets to deliver and then we might as well close up shop—if that's all right with you.'

'That's fine. In fact, I was going to suggest it myself.'

'Good. I'll call Billy and tell him to come in early for the deliveries. Oh, and I'll give my cousin a ring, too. Carolyn and I always do the town together come *mardi gras*.' She eyed Gabrielle speculatively. 'Why don't you come with us? You two would get along fine.'

Gabrielle shook her head. 'Thank you for asking. But I can't.'

'Come on, Gaby, *mardi gras* isn't any fun if you're alone.' Alma's eyes narrowed. 'Don't tell me you're plannin' to stay home all weekend.'

There was no getting around the truth. Gabrielle took a deep breath.

'I might. But not for the reasons you think.'

Alma put her hands on her hips. 'Nonsense. The reasons are always the same—you just don't want to meet people. I know you told me to mind my own business, but——'

'It isn't that.' The words were out before she could stop them. Alma looked at her in surprise, and Gabrielle touched her tongue to her lips. This was the first time she'd ever tried to answer the familiar accusation. 'It isn't that,' she said again, this time more softly. 'I—I want to meet people. It's just that—that there are things that happened back in New York ...' She fell silent.

'I wasn't tryin' to pry.' Alma's tone was gentle. 'But I hate to see you alone all the time. If some man broke your heart back home ...'

Gabrielle shook her head. 'It wasn't what you think. Things happened to me, and ...' She paused and her eyes met her assistant's. 'People use people.'

Her voice faded. What had ever possessed her to say that? It was as if meeting James was making all her carefully maintained defences crumble.

'Gaby,' Alma moved closer and put her hand on her friend's arm, 'you have to forget. Learn to trust again.'

Gabrielle smiled. 'I have,' she said. 'I trust you.'

'But not James?'

She hesitated, and her smile wavered a little. 'Remember when you asked how I managed to find James a hotel room?' she asked finally.

Alma nodded her head. 'Yes. But what does that have to do with——?'

'Well, I didn't find one. I mean, I couldn't. There wasn't a room anywhere.' She paused, then hurried on. 'So I took him home with me. James is staying at my house.'

There was a silence which was broken by Alma's gasping sound of disbelief. 'James Forrester? You took him...' Her eyes widened. 'My lord,' she whispered, her accent thickening, 'I don't believe it!'

Gabrielle shrugged her shoulders. 'I don't believe it, either,' she said with a forced laugh, 'but that's what I did. There didn't seem to be any other way.'

'Let me get this straight, Gaby. You're tellin' me that the man you never wanted to see again slept under your roof last night?'

'We spent hours trying to find him a room,' Gabrielle said defensively. 'What else could I have done? He was hurt and exhausted and...'

Alma threw her arms around Gabrielle and gave her a quick hug. 'I'm so glad.'

A scarlet glow crept into Gabrielle's cheeks. 'It's not what you think. It's just that James needed me. I couldn't turn away from him, could I?'

Alma's smile grew gentle. 'No, of course you couldn't. And how is he feelin' this mornin'?'

The image of James lying sprawled across the narrow bed, his skin tan against the white sheets, flickered in Gabrielle's mind again.

'I don't know,' she said, looking away from Alma's steady gaze. 'He was still sleeping when I left.'

'Well, then, you'd better hurry home before your patient wakes and finds his nurse missin'.'

Gabrielle turned towards her. 'Are you sure you don't mind? I can call James and tell him I'll be a while.'

The older woman shook her head. 'Go on home, Gaby,' she said gently. 'Get back to your patient before he wakes and finds his nurse gone. Here,' she added, plucking a rose from the vase beside her, 'give him this on his breakfast tray.' Her eyes twinkled. 'Just be sure and tell him it's from me.'

Outside, the sun beat down as if determined to make up for the recent days of poor weather. The early morning streets were unusually crowded as people gathered to begin the long holiday celebration.

Gabrielle almost regretted running this morning. When she'd awakened, she'd dressed automatically in shorts, T-shirt, and running shoes, but by the time she went down to check on James she'd begun to think about cancelling the run. Driving to the shop would be quicker.

But then she'd quietly pushed open his door and looked into the room. James had been lying on his belly, naked to where the blanket lay tangled across his hips. One leg—the injured one—was thrust out, tan against the white sheet. Pale sunlight dappled his skin, dusting his flesh with gold.

Her mouth had gone dry. Quickly, she'd stepped back into the hall and pulled the door shut. And then she'd scribbled a hasty note and let herself quietly out of the house, hoping that running would bring back her sense of equilibrium.

She wasn't naïve. She had attended an exclusive girls' day school. Her classmates were the daughters of wealthy men—bankers, lawyers, politicians—some of whose photos hung on Uncle Tony's walls.

'Respectable people,' he'd said with a throaty laugh as he wrote out the first tuition cheque and handed it to her father. 'Nothing's too good for our Gabriella, hey, Giovanni?'

The school prided itself on protecting its young charges from the real world. But its curriculum was thoroughly modern. Even the health classes offered the most up-to-date texts and films, and her teacher had been frank to the point of embarrassment.

'Remember, girls, there's always time to make a proper decision,' the woman had said during a discussion of sexuality. 'Your body readies itself slowly—we're more fortunate than men when it comes to such things. A knowledgeable young woman can never be rushed into something she'll later regret.'

It had all sounded reasonable, if somewhat mechanical. And it had proved accurate. Gabrielle had dated—a classmate's brother, a couple of boys she'd met at school dances, a few of the men at work—and she'd always had the time and the will to push away from their goodnight kisses before they deepened. The kisses, and the furtive touches of their hands, had been pleasant at best, but never anything more.

That wasn't the way things had been last night. Reason had fled while she was in James's arms, and there'd certainly been nothing slow about her body's reactions. Desire had been a white-hot flame, burning out of control. Gabrielle had dreamed about those moments all night, and then this morning, seeing him asleep...

She stumbled over a crack in the pavement. *Stupid, stupid, stupid.* Why hadn't she telephoned home from the shop? Waking James at a discreet distance would have been sensible. Well, it wasn't too late. The bakery was just ahead. She'd order coffee and the cakes, and while the clerk was filling the order she'd call James. There was a public phone just outside the shop...

...which was out of order. So much for her clever scheme, Gabrielle thought a little while later as she let herself quietly into the still silent house, the bakery bag clutched in her arms. She started to ease the door shut, then thought better of it and let it slam like a clap of thunder. She waited, heart racing. But the hall filled with silence.

She sighed as she walked into the kitchen. The juice and note were on the counter, untouched. All right, she'd make coffee and put the cakes in a warm oven. Maybe the smells of breakfast would awaken James. If not, she'd shower: the plumbing in the house was venerable and moaned and gurgled with age. If all that noise didn't do the trick, well, then she'd have no choice but to awaken him.

She worked quickly, measuring the coffee and pouring boiling water through it, setting out a basket for the cakes. Every now and then, she lifted her head and listened for sounds from the spare room, but there weren't any, and gradually her disappointment at his not being awake turned to worry.

Suppose James was ill? Suppose he had a fever? Suppose he'd got up while she was out and fallen?

Her heart tripped. Something terrible might have happened to him and here she was, hiding in the kitchen. Quickly, she hurried down the hall.

His door was still shut. Carefully, holding her breath, she opened it and looked inside the room.

James seemed to be sleeping soundly. He was lying on his back, both arms thrown above his head, his chest rising and falling steadily. Gabrielle's gaze moved swiftly over the patches of dark hair in his armpits, to the mat of it across his chest, then to the flat ridges of muscle in his abdomen. A shadowy arrow led down from his navel, dipping below the blanket that lay across his groin.

'James?' Her whisper hung in the still air. She cleared her throat. 'James?' Her voice was louder this time, but he didn't move.

What now? The answer was obvious. Now, she had to cross the room to his side, put her hand on his arm, touch him . . .

'No!'

She started, shocked by the raw sound of his voice. The word sounded as if it had been torn from his throat.

'James? Are you——?'

'No,' he cried again. His eyes were closed tight, his face contorted. Suddenly, his arms shot into the air, his hands closing on something unseen. 'Gabrielle. Gabrielle!'

She reached him just as he sat up abruptly, his back against the headboard.

'James. James, wake up,' she said, putting her hand on his shoulder.

His eyes opened. His stare was empty and unfocused. Then, as she said his name again, he turned towards her and his gaze steadied.

'Gabrielle?' he said in a hoarse whisper.

'Yes.' She smiled. 'It's all right, James. You just had a bad dream.'

He stared at her, then ran his hand through his hair, pushing the dark locks back from his brow.

'What time is it?'

'It's still early. How does your knee feel?'

James shifted his leg free of the sheet. 'I think the swelling's gone down. Why don't you check?'

Later, she wanted to say, I'll check later, when you're out of bed and safely in the kitchen, when you're dressed, when my heart isn't skittering so crazily.

But the innocent look on his face couldn't hide the laughter in his eyes. He was teasing her, and she determined not to give away anything more than she already had.

'I'll be glad to.'

James let go of her wrist and she leaned forward and gently began unwrapping the bandage that covered his knee. She tried not to touch him, but it was impossible not to feel the warmth of his skin beneath her fingers. Her hand shook as she pulled the last of the bandage away—and then the sight of his swollen, discoloured knee drove everything else from her mind. The memory of that single moment in the car the day before, when she'd looked at him and wondered if his pain was really as bad as it had seemed, rose in her throat like bile.

'Oh, James,' she whispered, 'it looks awful.' Her eyes met his. 'It must hurt something fierce.'

He put his hand to her cheek. 'Don't look so worried,' he said softly. 'It always looks a hell of a lot worse than it feels.'

'Are you sure? Did you use the ice pack I gave you last night? Let me refill it and get you some aspirin. Let me call the hospital and ask——'

'Gabrielle, I'm fine, really.' Her eyes spoke her doubt, and he smiled. 'Watch,' he said, and in one swift motion he swung his legs to the floor, the sheet falling carelessly across his loins.

His face paled beneath his tan. Gabrielle put her hand on his arm.

'James, you're pushing things. Stay in bed for a while. I'll bring your breakfast to you.'

He shook his head. 'No.' His voice was hard; he drew a breath, then let it out slowly. 'No,' he repeated, this time with a tight smile. 'The best thing is exercise. If I baby it, my knee will just freeze up.'

'Are you sure?'

He nodded. 'What I need is coffee. The smell of it's driving me crazy.'

His colour was returning. Still, Gabrielle hesitated. 'Can you get yourself dressed?' she asked.

James laughed. 'What would you do if I said I couldn't?'

She felt a rush of heat to her cheeks, but she met his gaze. 'I'd call my neighbour,' she said evenly. 'Miss Toner is seventy years old, but she'd be glad to help.'

He grinned. 'We'll let Miss Toner off this time. I'll manage by myself. I think I'll even try the shower.'

'Just be careful, James. Please.'

He nodded as he wrapped the sheet around him and knotted it at the hip. 'If you'd just hand me those crutches—that's it.' He stood up carefully. 'Stop looking so worried. I promise, I won't slip and drown.'

Gabrielle smiled. 'You'd better not. I can just see myself trying to explain that to Nurse Ramrod.'

James's laughter echoed after her as she walked from the room and closed the door after her. It was an infectious sound, and by the time she climbed the stairs to the next floor and her own room she was laughing too.

It was the first time she'd begun the day with laughter in longer than she could remember.

When she came downstairs again, her hair still damp from the shower, Gabrielle was dressed in a loose white cotton pullover and white cotton drawstring trousers. James was in the kitchen, one crutch tucked beneath his arm, wearing faded jeans and an equally faded sweatshirt.

He smiled as she entered the room. 'I managed the shower and the clothing,' he said. 'But shaving is something else.' He winced as he touched his fingers to his bruised jaw. 'Can you survive the sight of me with a beard?'

Her heart leaped as she looked at him. He looked, she thought, sexy and dangerous. It was a combination she had never thought she'd face over the breakfast table.

She turned away quickly and reached for cups and saucers.

'No problem,' she said lightly. 'What do you think about having breakfast on the terrace?'

'I'm one hobble ahead of you, landlady.' James grinned and motioned to the door that led outside. 'I've already set the table. And before you ask, I downed two aspirin with my juice.'

She smiled. 'Good. I was going to threaten not to let you have any *beignets* unless you did.'

James grinned wickedly. 'Too late. I sneaked a couple while I was waiting.' His smile faded as his eyes moved over her. 'The waiting was worthwhile,' he said softly. 'You look beautiful.'

Her hand went to her hair in a self-conscious gesture. Their eyes met and she touched her tongue to her lips.

'Thank you.'

He smiled, but his eyes were solemn. 'You're welcome.'

Gabrielle swallowed drily. 'Why don't you—why don't you go on outside? I'll bring the coffee and the cakes.'

The terrace was small and very private, shut off from the rest of the courtyard by a high brick wall overgrown with ivy. James had set out china and silver, even linen napkins he'd found in the drawer. Alma's rose stood in a goblet in the centre of the table.

'I see you found Alma's gift.' Gabrielle nodded at the flower as she poured coffee. 'She says to tell you she hopes you feel better soon.'

'Nice lady,' he said with a relaxed smile, and then he took a sip of coffee. 'Umm, this is good. Is it the chicory blend?'

'Yes. Do you like it?'

He nodded. 'Very much. I could get used to New Orleans cuisine without any trouble at all.'

Gabrielle smiled. 'Good, because I'm going to try my hand at jambalaya tonight. I'll go out later while you nap. I'll pick up some shrimp and tomatoes...'

'No.' She looked up in surprise. James's voice was as hard as his eyes. He drew a breath, then smiled tightly. 'Not without me, I mean. You don't think I'm going to stay cooped up during Carnival, do you?'

'But your knee, James. The hospital said you were supposed to rest.'

This time, his smile was the boyish one she remembered. 'Well, I did. I rested all night.' He put his cup down and sat forward. 'If you're determined to make an invalid of me, we'll drive. That way I can sit and still see what's going on.'

'The traffic will be impossible. Alma says——'

'It doesn't matter. We're not in a rush, are we? And if we see something that looks interesting, we'll park and take a closer look.'

Gabrielle looked doubtful. 'You're forgetting about my little Toyota, aren't you? After an hour, you'll probably beg me to drop you off at the hospital.'

James grinned. 'Which is why I telephoned the car rental people while you were upstairs.' He bit into a cake, then swallowed. 'Would you believe they've agreed to let me try my hand at auto demolition again?'

She laughed. 'No, I would not.'

'Well, they did. I explained that I needed a car, that it would be hard to get to them with my knee all banged up, and they said not to worry, they'd have someone deliver a car to me here this morning.'

Gabrielle looked at him warily. 'Hertz is going to do that?'

James looked down at his coffee. 'Yes. Why not?'

'You're a terrible liar, James Forrester.'

His head came up and he stared at her. 'What does that mean?'

'Come on, you know what it means. You could probably charm the catfish out of the Mississippi if you wanted. Just look at the scam you pulled on the hospital.' She laughed softly. 'Letting them think I was going to take care of you—honestly, James, that was awful.'

He leaned back in his chair and smiled. 'Not so awful. Look where it got me.'

'Yes, look where it got you.' She laughed again. 'In other words, deceit *does* pay.'

She waited for his answering smile, but it never came. Instead, he tucked the crutch beneath his arm, got to his feet, and hobbled across the terrace to stare over the wall at the courtyard.

'If there's no other choice, it does,' he said, his voice flat.

'Hey,' Gabrielle said softly, 'I was only teasing. I...'

James turned towards her. 'Sometimes the end justifies the means,' he said, watching her. 'I mean, if something is important enough, the way you get it doesn't really matter.' His eyes narrowed. 'You can agree with that.'

She looked at him questioningly. The conversation had somewhere taken a turn. They'd gone from pleasant banter to dark riddles, although she had no idea why.

'James? What is it?'

He stared at her, then looked away again. 'Nothing. Nothing—I'm just tired.'

Gabrielle rose slowly. 'Maybe you injured yourself more than you realised.'

'I'm fine.'

'Are you sure? Did they do X-rays and blood tests and...'

James turned towards her. 'Believe me, the doctors examined every inch of my body.'

'Are you sure?'

He smiled. 'Yes. And Nurse Ramrod checked again, just to make sure they hadn't missed anything. That woman knows more about me than my mother.'

'Which puts her light years ahead of me.' Gabrielle drew a breath. 'I don't know anything about you, James. Do you realise that?'

He hobbled back to the table and sank into his chair. 'OK,' he said easily, 'what would you like to know?'

'Well, you never mentioned why you were in New Orleans...'

'Didn't I?'

Gabrielle shook her head. 'No. I assumed you were on vacation, but...'

He sat back and smiled at her. 'Good assumption. I *am* on vacation—I always wanted to see *mardi gras*. What else?'

She gave him a quick smile. 'I don't know exactly. Little things. Where you're from. What you do for a living...'

His eyes met hers. 'I'm disappointed, Gabrielle.'

'Disappointed? Why?'

'Such prosaic questions,' he said, reaching for her hand and lifting it to his lips. 'I was hoping you'd ask about the important things?'

'The important things?'

James nodded and the ghost of a smile tilted across his mouth. 'Of course. Do I have a wife stashed somewhere? Do I have the requisite one point five kiddies and a cottage in the suburbs?'

It was impossible not to smile in return. 'All right,' she said, 'do you?'

'Do I what?' he asked, feigning an expression of innocence.

Gabrielle laughed. 'Do you have a wife, one point five kiddies, and a cottage in the suburbs?'

He grinned. 'No, no, and no. And—just to save you the trouble of asking—all my parts are in good working order, except for this damned knee, I like spring picnics and summer rain, I think whoever invented opera did it just to confuse good music and bad theatre, and no one's painted anything worth a damn since Degas.' His fingers laced through hers and he looked into her eyes. 'And I think you're the most beautiful woman I've ever met. Now, is there anything else you need to know?'

Gabrielle felt dazzled with happiness. 'No,' she said softly. 'I don't think there is.'

Suddenly, lines appeared beside his mouth, and his expression grew grim.

'Promise me you'll always remember that.'

Her smiled dimmed. 'James? What...?'

'Promise me,' he said urgently.

She looked at him, seeing once again the dark shadows and the livid flesh beside the stitches across his cheek, and she nodded.

'All right,' she whispered, 'I promise.'

James stared back at her, then leaned across the table and kissed her. His kiss was tender at the start and then, with a swiftness that left her breathless, he cupped her face in his hands and his kiss deepened, became more impassioned and somehow more poignant than she'd ever thought a kiss could be.

An explosion of light blossomed behind her closed eyelids. She felt it shimmer like a white flame that invaded her mind and body. Her lips parted beneath his; she moaned softly and wound her arms around his neck, whispering his name against his mouth like an incantation for the spell she was falling under.

The shrill ring of the doorbell shattered the magic and they separated. James's eyes held Gabrielle's as he smoothed dark strands of silken hair from her cheeks.

'Who...?' She swallowed. 'I wasn't expecting anyone.'

James smiled. 'It's probably for me. The car rental people said they'd make delivery within the hour.' He kissed her and got to his feet. 'I'll be right back.'

Gabrielle nodded. She watched as he hobbled into the kitchen, watched until he vanished into the shadowy hallway, and then she leaned back in her chair and closed her eyes.

A little while ago, she'd told Alma she'd taken James in because he needed her.

The truth was more complicated.

A few days ago, James had been a stranger to be feared and avoided. Now, it was she who needed him. She longed for his kisses, for his presence—and for the moment she could tell him she was falling in love with him.

CHAPTER EIGHT

A FIRE-ENGINE-RED Corvette was parked at the door of the carriage house.

James was straight-faced when he marched Gabrielle to the kerb and showed the car to her, but the laughter in his eyes gave him away.

'The boy who dropped it off said the manager told him to say they were awfully sorry, but they were out of sedans.' He smiled and looped his arm lightly around her shoulders. 'I told him we'd do our best not to be too distressed.'

'It's a lovely car, James. But your knee—are you sure you're up to a drive?'

He smiled. 'When I injured it in college, my mother was determined to take me home and keep me in bed until it was healed.' He shifted the single crutch he was using, and he and Gabrielle started slowly through the courtyard to the house. 'My father insisted I stay at school and keep moving. I preferred my mother's plan, of course...'

'Of course?'

There was a brief silence and then James laughed. 'My father was—is—a man who believes you measure success by how many awards you've won or how many dollars you've earned. I was up for an athletic trophy and he was sure I'd lose it if I gave in to the injury.'

Gabrielle looked at him as they entered the house. 'So you stayed at school?'

James shook his head. 'No. I went home. And after a couple of days of being pampered, the knee froze up completely.' He started down the hall to his room. 'So

111

I took my father's advice, went back to school, and kept moving—all of which would have been fine, except it meant admitting he'd been right in the first place.'

'And that was hard to do,' Gabrielle said with a questioning smile.

He nodded. 'Yes. Always. We're different people, the old man and me. We have different goals and...' he paused and looked at her '...and it still amazes me when I realise that, in many ways, he's known me better than I've known myself.'

A curious flatness had crept into his voice. 'James? Is something the matter?'

His eyes met hers, then slid away. 'No. No, nothing. It's getting late, that's all, and if we're not careful this special day is going to slip by.' Smiling, he opened the bedroom door. 'You have five minutes to get ready, Nurse Shelton. Can you manage?'

Gabrielle laughed and touched her hand to her hair. 'Not if I'm going to put on some make-up and fix my hair and...'

James's smile tilted crookedly across his face. 'What could you possibly do that would make you more beautiful than you already are?' he said softly, and the door closed quietly after him.

An hour later, James had traded his crutches for a cane. 'These things have to go,' he'd said impatiently as he settled behind the wheel of the Corvette. 'They're much too restrictive.'

Gabrielle smiled at him. 'You're not likely to play football today,' she said gently.

There was no answering smile. 'You never know what you're going to have to do,' he said tersely, pulling out from the kerb. 'Just tell me where I can find a surgical pharmacy.'

It took time to find a cane long enough to suit his height, but, once he'd found the right one, he was surprisingly agile. His knee hurt despite all his bravado—

Gabrielle saw the skin whiten around his mouth when he first put his weight on the injured leg—but after a few steps he was smiling.

'See? I'm good as new. Now, where would you like to go?'

'Some place where you won't do any walking,' she said quickly. 'Please, James, promise me that.'

She needn't have worried. The streets of the city were thronged with revellers. The French Quarter was all but impassable, by car as well as on foot. The crowds were thick along the Rampart Street parade route.

'No crowds,' James muttered, and Gabrielle breathed a sigh of relief. He tapped his fingers lightly against the steering-wheel, then turned to her. 'Any suggestions?'

'We could go back to the carriage house,' she said.

He frowned. 'There'll probably be wall to wall people on your street by now.'

'Will it matter? I mean, will the noise bother you, or...?'

His eyes met hers. 'I told you, I don't like crowds.'

His voice was sharp. Of course, she thought, he was tired already, but he wasn't about to admit it.

'Well then, why don't we get out of the city altogether? Alma once mentioned River Road—she says there are some beautiful plantations along the banks of the river. I'll bet they're all but deserted today.'

James's eyebrows rose. 'Plantations?'

Gabrielle laughed. 'That's exactly what I said to Alma. But she swears they exist.'

'Well, let's go find out.'

The River Road followed the twists and bends of the sluggish Mississippi. It was an old highway, one that had in past times wound its way from plantation to plantation, and, as Alma had promised, many of the big houses were still standing, some in majestic splendour, others in brooding decay.

'After a while, you'll expect to see Rhett Butler, waitin' at the side of the road,' Alma had said, 'a mint julep in his hand and his eyes smilin' just for you.'

Gabrielle glanced across the car at James. Never mind the mint juleps or Rhett Butler, she thought with a little shiver of excitement, the man beside her was all she wanted.

The day was warm. Out here, near the river, the air was hot and humid, thick with the promise of summertime. James had taken off his tweed jacket and tossed it into the back of the car. He'd changed his sweatshirt for a long-sleeved, cream-coloured shirt which he wore with the sleeves rolled up. Sunlight danced along his muscled forearms. The top buttons of the shirt were undone, and she could see dark whorls of hair curling out from beneath the soft fabric. He was wearing the mirrored sunglasses that had so angered her when they'd first met, but now they only added to the aura of rugged masculinity that emanated from him. The car windows were open, and the breeze played with his hair, tossing the dark locks across his forehead.

He was as handsome as any wicked-eyed riverboat gambler from the past, a dazzling combination of charm and good looks, strength and gentleness. He was a man women dreamed of, and he was here, with her, smiling at her, talking to her, touching her hand as it lay in her lap.

The thought of it took her breath away. When had she last felt this happy?

Not in years, she thought, putting her head back and closing her eyes, not even before her father's illness or the nightmare that had followed. She'd never smiled as much, or laughed as much—not since she was a little girl.

She'd been happy then. Her growing-up years had been filled with laughter, despite the fact that she'd lost her mother. Her father—and Uncle Tony—had been all the warm and loving family she'd needed. But as she'd grown older, her life had undergone a subtle change. She had been excluded from the little cliques and secret sororities at school. She knew it had had something to do with her father's connection with Vitale, but there was nothing she could do about it. Her father had explained things to her. Powerful men, like Tony Vitale, were envied and feared.

It was as simple as that. It had to be. Because if it wasn't, if there was a shred of truth to the rumours, then what did that make of her father?

'Gabrielle?'

She started as she felt the weight of his hand on hers. It seemed to take great effort to open her eyes and look at him.

'Yes, James.'

His gaze moved over her face. 'What's wrong? You seem so far away.'

She felt the harsh pressure of past unshed tears in her eyes and she turned her head before he saw them, too.

'I was just thinking,' she said slowly. 'This morning, when you talked about your father, you said he knew you better than you knew yourself.' She paused, swallowed, then looked at him again. 'But what about knowing him? I mean, do you really know the kind of man he is?'

His jaw tightened. 'I thought I did,' he said after a while. 'But I'm beginning to think I was wrong.' He glanced at her and smiled tightly. 'When you're a kid, you see things in black and white. Fathers are good or bad, that's all. It's only when you grow up that you realise they're people, that they can be both good and bad, just like the rest of us.'

A sob caught in Gabrielle's throat. James looked at her, then drove to an easy stop on the shoulder of the road. She came into his arms in a rush, her face buried against his chest.

'What is it?' he demanded, tilting her face up to his and looking into her eyes. 'Gabrielle?'

She shook her head. 'Nothing,' she whispered. 'I just thought about my father. I wish I could tell him I love him again, that nothing could ever make me stop, no matter what he—no matter who...'

A muscle moved in James's jaw. 'I'm sure he knows that, somehow.' He bent to her and kissed her mouth. When he drew away, she sighed and smiled tremulously.

'I'm sorry,' she said. 'I don't know what's the matter with me. I haven't thought about the past at all, and suddenly, today...'

James put his hand lightly over her lips. 'This isn't the time to talk about the past, Gabrielle.'

'But you said...'

His mouth narrowed. 'I know what I said. But today— today is special. It belongs to us.' He stared into her eyes, and finally a smile eased across his face. 'And you know what? Let's begin living it to the hilt right now.'

A ferry took them across the river to an old plantation called Belle Hélène. They walked the grounds of Nottoway Plantation and then, in the late afternoon, they drove slowly along narrow back roads. Cultivated fields stretched away on either side; cabins stood half hidden in groves of live oak trees, smoke rising lazily from their chimneys. Dogs rushed out, barking furiously; strangers smiled and waved as if Gabrielle and James were old friends.

The Corvette had become a time machine, taking them back to gentler days, to a past that seemed simple and without blemish. But the present was different. What would James say when he found out that the woman beside him was really Gabrielle Chiari, a woman hiding a tangled past? Would he look at her differently?

When dusk fell, they pulled up before a graceful plantation house set well back from the road. White columns rose from its porch to its roof; soft strains of music drifted on the still-warm evening air.

Gabrielle looked at James as he shut off the engine. 'Where are we?' she whispered, as if a too loud voice might break the spell.

He laughed softly, and she knew that he, too, was caught up in the magic. 'Tara, for all I know. There's a discreet sign that says this is a restaurant. Shall we try it?'

She looked doubtful. 'What about the way we're dressed?'

His eyes darkened as he looked at her. 'I'll put my jacket on,' he said, and he laid his hand against her cheek. 'As for you—you're far too beautiful to be turned away.'

A smiling woman dressed in a nineteenth-century hoop-skirted gown led them to a secluded table in the far corner of the main room. Candles flickered everywhere, their dazzling golden light reflected in the bubbled glass of the old mirror above the marble fireplace and in the Moët et Chandon champagne James ordered. When the waiter brought them menus, Gabrielle shook her head.

'You choose for me,' she said to James.

His eyes met hers, and a strange half-smile twisted over his mouth.

'Are you sure you want to entrust yourself to me?'

Her heart turned over. They were talking about much more than dinner, she thought, and she wanted to reach across the table and put her hand against his lips.

Instead, she nodded.

'Yes,' she whispered, and even the waiter smiled.

She had no idea what it was she ate. It was all delicious and elegantly served, but Gabrielle had eyes only for the man opposite her. Everything James said was clever, every motion of his hands graceful. The sound of his voice touched her with pleasure.

'James.' He looked at her and she touched her tongue to her lips. 'I just wanted you to know how happy I am. Thank you. Thank you for changing my life. I was so—so lost before, so unhappy...'

His eyes grew dark. 'Don't.'

The anguish in his voice startled her. 'Have I embarrassed you? I didn't mean to.'

'Gabrielle, please.' She stared at him and he drew in his breath. 'Come,' he whispered, pushing back his chair, 'dance with me.'

'We can't,' she said, 'your knee...'

She looked into his eyes, then took his hand and walked with him to the empty dance-floor. James's arms went around her and she settled against him, her head pressed to his shoulder, and they swayed slowly to the music.

'Gabrielle.'

There was an urgency in his voice, and she looked up at him, trying to read his eyes, but his face was in shadow.

'What is it? Are you feeling ill? Forgive me—I've been selfish. It's your leg, isn't it?'

His arms tightened around her. 'My leg's fine. I just wanted to say your name and tell you again that this day has been special.'

Special. A special day for Gabrielle Shelton and James Forrester. But she wasn't Gabrielle Shelton, and it was time he knew that. It was past time.

'James,' she said, her voice slurred with her need to strip away the falsehoods that separated them, 'we have to talk.'

His mouth narrowed. 'No.' His voice was terse. 'Talking's the last thing we want to do.'

'We have to, James. Please.'

He put her from him. 'No.' His tone was sharp, and, when she looked at him in surprise, he drew a breath and turned away from her. 'It's getting late,' he said. 'It's time we left. Give me a moment to settle our bill.'

Silently, she followed him back to their table. She would do as he'd asked, she thought, but only until they got outside. In the darkness, the truth about herself would be easier to tell.

Later, remembering, she would be staggered by her own folly.

In her eagerness to end her deception, it never occurred to her to wonder why James, who only last night had been so insistent on facing the past, was now equally determined to bury it.

But then, James had known all along where talking would lead them.

Outside, silver clouds rolled across the moon, hiding it from view. The rising fog was like a curtain, obscuring the house and everything around it. By the time they reached the car, they were cut off from the world.

Gabrielle put her hand on his arm. 'Please,' she said, her voice low, husky with nervousness, 'let's talk here, in the dark. This is hard for me to say.'

He shook his head. 'I told you, I don't want to hear it.'

'Yesterday, you said no one could run from the past.'

'Leave it alone, dammit! Just——'

She drew in her breath. 'We have to talk about who we are. We really don't know anything about each other.'

His hands framed her face and lifted it to his. In the shadowed night, his features were indistinct. She felt the warmth of his breath as he spoke.

'We know all we need to know, Gabrielle.'

'But there are things that might change the way you——'

'Listen to me.' His voice held a rough urgency. 'As far as I'm concerned, our lives began last night.'

She wanted to believe him. But he'd told her to face the past squarely, and she knew that that was what had to be done.

She had only been kidding herself the last few months. She didn't really believe Tony Vitale wanted her silenced, but there were other things to fear. All it would take to resurrect the past was a sharp-eyed reporter or a persistent federal agent to discover her whereabouts.

'You have to listen to me, James. When I—when I lived in New York...'

He shook his head impatiently. 'I don't give a damn about New York. Just tell me that you've left it behind.'

She hesitated. 'I—I think I have. But I'm not sure. I...'

His breath hissed between his teeth. 'What do you mean, you're not sure?'

There was so much to explain. If only she knew where to begin, how to tell him her story.

'I meant that—that you can't just walk away from the past, James. You can't shed it like an old skin.'

'You can.' His voice was sharp. 'The life you left in New York, the one I left in Washington, are meaningless. You and I——'

Gabrielle stared at him. 'Is that where you're from? Washington?'

It was James who hesitated this time. 'Yes,' he said finally. 'But never mind that now. Why did you say——?'

'Do you realise, that's the first thing you've told me about yourself? What do you do in Washington?' She waited for his answer, but he said nothing. Nervous laughter rose in her throat. 'Just don't tell me you work for the government.'

'Gabrielle, please...'

Somehow, the night had become strange and alien. She shivered as it closed down around them. What she'd said had been meant as a joke, but suddenly there was nothing funny about it.

When they'd met, she'd wondered if James meant her harm. She'd even wondered if he was a reporter. But the possibility that he might be an agent had never occurred to her.

No. Not James.

'Answer my question,' she said. 'What do you do in Washington?'

'Does it matter?'

Her spine grew rigid. 'If you work for the government—if you're part of that slime...'

She felt a sudden tension grip his body. 'All right.' His voice was grim. 'If you insist upon resurrecting the past, we'll do it somewhere private. Get in the car.'

Gabrielle shuddered in the cool night air. James was frightening her; he reminded her of how he'd been that morning in the alley.

'We can talk right here,' she said.

His hands closed on her shoulders. 'Get in the car. Now.'

His voice was like a whip. She tried to step back, but his fingers bit into her flesh. A chill raced along her skin.

'You can't talk to me like that, James.'

He laughed unpleasantly. 'It's a little late to tell me what I can and can't do, isn't it?'

'What do you mean?'

'I've done whatever I wanted from the minute we met. Why should that change now?'

'James,' her voice was thin, 'what's wrong with you? Why are you acting this way?'

'I'm even living in your house.'

'James, stop this.'

'What kind of damn fool thing was that to do, huh? Inviting a man home when you don't even know him.'

Gabrielle drew a shallow breath. 'Stop it,' she whispered. 'I don't know why you want to scare me, but you are. It isn't very——'

'It's a little late to be scared, don't you think? The time for that was *before* you asked a stranger into your home.'

The moon escaped its clouded prison. In the sudden pale light, she saw the terrible purpose in his face.

Don't panic, she told herself, even though her heart was hammering, don't panic. This is James, this is the man who kissed you and held you, the man who saved your life.

'You aren't a stranger,' she said, her eyes meeting his. 'Not any more.'

Her words had been meant to calm him. Instead, they seemed to enrage him. He cursed sharply, then pulled her tightly against him, holding her so that she felt the steel of his hard body.

'Of course I'm a stranger,' he snarled. 'Dammit, woman, are you a fool?'

Tears rose in her eyes. 'Why are you doing this?'

'Why didn't you ask me any questions the morning we met?'

'Questions? What kind of——?'

'Where I was from. Who I was. Why didn't you ask?'

'I don't know. It didn't seem important.'

'All you asked was what I'd been doing in the alley and how I knew the name of your shop. I gave you some idiotic answers, and you bought them.'

The terror she'd fought to suppress burst free, beating dark wings within her breast.

'Who are you?' she whispered.

James imprisoned her head in his hands, his fingers tangling in her hair. His eyes swept over her face, lingering on her parted lips.

'I tried,' he said. 'God, I tried. I thought we could play it your way. I told myself we could bury the past and pretend it never happened.' He moved closer to her, until his face was all she could see. 'Hell, I should have known it wouldn't work.'

'James, I swear, if you don't let me go...'

He laughed. 'What will you do?' His voice was cold. 'Scream? Go on, give it your best. No one will hear you.'

Gabrielle stared into his eyes. The pale chips of icy blue chilled her soul. Suddenly she slammed her hands against his chest. He did nothing to stop her, and she beat at him until finally she slumped against him, sobbing and exhausted.

'I hate you, James Forrester,' she panted. 'I hate you, I——'

She cried out as he pulled her to him. 'No, you don't,' he said through his teeth, 'you damn well don't.'

His mouth fell on hers, and he lifted her to her toes so that her body was pressed fully against his. His teeth nipped sharply into the soft flesh of her bottom lip. She gasped, and instantly he thrust his tongue into her mouth, filling her with the taste and heat of him.

He moaned her name against her mouth, then pressed his lips to the long curve of her throat.

'Don't,' she whispered. 'Please.'

She was trembling in his arms. A heat was rising within her, moving like wildfire through her blood, turning her limbs to jelly. James's kisses were warm against her skin; her head fell back and her hands slid under his sweater and up his chest, her palms flattening against his skin, her pulse racing, racing...

'Gabrielle.' The urgency in his voice brought her back.

Her lashes lifted slowly and she looked into his eyes. They were smoky, clouded with desire.

'I know who you are,' he said softly.

Her heart skittered wildly against her ribs. 'What do you mean?'

He smiled, and she knew that the memory of the terrible sadness of that smile would last her the remainder of her life.

He watched her face, watched the passion leave her eyes, watched first dismay and then fear move over her features, and he made a sound that was half-laugh, half-groan.

'You're Gabrielle Chiari.'

The world seemed to stop spinning. The moon hung still against a painted sky, and Gabrielle's breath caught in her throat.

'What do you want with me?'

James's lips drew back from his teeth. 'You fool,' he whispered. 'Nobody walks away from Tony Vitale.'

CHAPTER NINE

THERE were certain universal truths that had no basis in reality but were valid all the same.

Some were grounded in superstition: if you closed your eyes, whatever frightened you would disappear.

Others were more sophisticated: if you travelled to some new place, it took far less time to return home than it did to get there.

Gabrielle knew both beliefs were childish. Still, on this muggy night in the Louisiana Delta, they were both applicable.

No matter how tightly she closed her eyes, each time she opened them James was still seated beside her in the dark, leather-scented interior of the Corvette, his face set in stone. And the miles were ticking away with impossible rapidity. James had abandoned the country lanes for the highway, and they were hurtling through the night, passing slower-moving cars with an abandon that left her breathless.

Not that it mattered. If she had to die, better in a twisted mass of metal than...than...

Gabrielle choked back a sob. No. No matter what James had said, no matter how it had sounded, he hadn't meant—he couldn't have meant...

Nobody walks away from Tony Vitale.

The words were so melodramatic they were almost laughable. But James hadn't laughed when he'd said them: his eyes had been the colour of winter ice, the lines of his mouth and jaw like granite.

125

What had she said to him? 'Are you crazy?' It had to have been something like that, because she could still remember his answer.

'Yes,' he'd whispered, 'that's exactly what I am.'

And then, before she could say anything else, he'd caught her by the arm and started forcing her into the car. She'd screamed then, her voice rising eerily into the muggy night. James had pulled her to him and put his mouth to her ear.

'Don't.' The ominously whispered word, coupled with the twisting pressure of his hand on her wrist, had silenced her. She'd stood, trembling, in his embrace, and finally he'd drawn away just enough so he could look into her face. 'If you do as I say, it will be easier.'

His eyes had swept over her and he'd smiled, and for that brief moment she'd seen the man she knew.

'James.' Her whisper had been thin as air. 'James, please, please tell me . . .'

He'd smiled again, sadly this time, and gently stroked back the dark hair that had fallen over her cheek.

'I will, I'll tell you everything. But not here. Now, get into the car.'

And she had. There was nothing else she could do: the night was dark, the setting desolate, and, despite his injured knee, James was far stronger than she.

It made no sense. If James was supposed to kill her, he could have done it a dozen times over.

Unless . . .

She remembered how she'd trembled in his arms a little while ago, even after he'd said things that had terrified her, how her mouth had sought his despite the fear racing through her blood.

Were they both victims of some twisted passion that had nothing to do with love? Was that what had kept James from doing his job, was he taking her back to the carriage house so he could first take her body and then her life?

They reached the house and James pulled to the kerb. The car filled with silence as he switched off the engine. The street was surprisingly quiet for such a festive night, and it was ominously dark, with lengthened shadows from the distant street-light stretching ahead.

She felt a strange sense of displacement, as if she were here in mind but not in spirit, the same way she'd felt the night her father had died. The sound of music and laughter drifted to her faintly on the humid air, adding to the feeling that she had somehow become separated from the rest of the world.

James stirred beside her. 'When I open your door, I want you to get out of the car quickly. Do you understand.'

Gabrielle swallowed. Her mouth was dry; her tongue felt thick and it seemed to take great effort to answer him.

'James. James, whatever you're going to do— whatever you think you must do...'

But he wasn't listening. He stepped from the Corvette, the door closing softly after him. She watched as he stood still for a moment, looking first at the street and then at the night-draped courtyard, and she thought of a wild animal returning to its lair, checking it for intruders before entering. Her eyes followed his, trying to see the scene as he must, and suddenly the familiar street became frightening.

What was he watching for? The police? But they had no knowledge of Gabrielle Chiari and Tony Vitale. This was New Orleans, not New York.

Her door opened. James held his hand out to her.

'Let's go,' he said softly.

Like a woman in a dream, Gabrielle put her hand in his and stepped from the car. James slipped his arm around her; she felt the firm pressure of his hand against her hip, the solid press of his body at hip and thigh.

'Stay close to me,' he murmured.

As if she had a choice, she thought. His arm was a band of steel curved around her, moulding her against him.

'James.' Her voice was low-pitched. 'James, please, if only you'd listen.'

'I'll listen all you want once we're inside.'

She shook her head. 'It'll be too late then, James,' she said, holding herself stiff, trying to stop their implacable progress towards the dark courtyard. 'Don't you see?'

'Just keep moving. I think we're all right out here, on the street. It's too open, too visible. But I'll be damned if I'm going to take any chances I don't have to take. Move, dammit. Don't fight me.'

She stumbled as he propelled her forward, through the wrought-iron gate and into the courtyard. A tendril of Spanish moss brushed against her face, its touch damp and unearthly, and she shuddered. Wisps of fog rose from the overgrown garden that separated the main house from the carriage house, wraith-like in the darkness.

'James—listen to me.'

She cried out softly as he clamped his hand hard around hers.

'Not a sound,' he growled. 'Have you got that?'

Tears rose in her eyes and spilled down her cheeks. 'James, I beg you, don't do this. Don't hurt me.'

He stared at her. 'Gabrielle...'

'I thought that you—that we...'

In one swift motion, he pulled her into his arms, his mouth parting hers for a quick, dizzying kiss. She heard the pounding of her blood in her ears, felt the thud of her heart, and then James put her from him.

'Trust me, Gabrielle.'

The husky plea made her want to weep and laugh at the same time. She *had* trusted him, that was how he had trapped her in the first place. They both knew that.

He had just chided her for it—did he really expect her to be stupid enough to make the same mistake again?

Or did he think the dark fascination that bound them together would make her compliant, even in the face of her own death?

'Open the door.' She stared at him and his voice turned harsh with impatience. 'Come on, dammit, get your key out and open the door.'

She did as he'd ordered. The door swung open while her mind scampered in a frantic race for answers. They moved slowly through the foyer and into the living-room. There had to be something she could do, something...

She kicked out at him as the door closed after them. The cane spun out of his hand and clattered to the floor. He swore and she kicked again, her foot connecting with his knee. She heard the air spill from his lungs and knew he'd been hurt. He groaned her name. The sound was a knife twisting in her heart, but she had no choice, she had to stop him, and she kicked out at him again.

He went down, gasping for breath. 'Gabrielle—you don't understand.'

She stood over him, breathless, tears flooding her eyes, watching as he rose slowly to one knee. He was in pain: his moon-washed face was contorted, and the effort it took to rise was in his eyes.

He was an easy target now, no danger to her, not while he was like this.

Kick him again, her mind screamed. Get the poker from the fireplace and hit him with it. Open the door and run screaming from the house.

'Gabrielle?'

The sound of his voice stunned her. All the questions a man had ever asked a woman were in the way he whispered her name. He grunted, drew a deep breath, and rose to his feet.

It was too late now. He was whole again, strong and powerful as he towered over her. Her heart skipped a beat, then began to race like an insane clock.

'Who are you, James?' she said hoarsely, her eyes on his face. 'At least tell me that.'

He stared at her while an eternity slipped by, and then a smile transformed his face, changing it from that of a stranger to that of the man she knew.

'I'm the man who's going to make love to you,' he whispered, and took her in his arms.

He bent to her and kissed her, his mouth warm, open, and wet against hers. She trembled as his arms tightened around her, moaned as he bent her backwards, his mouth still on hers. His hand moved over her with rough urgency and her blood surged in response.

'Don't,' she groaned.

He lifted her to him until she was pressed against the length of his body. His heart thundered against her breast; his flesh quickened and rose against the cradling warmth of her loins. She shuddered as his hands cupped her buttocks.

'Gabrielle,' he whispered, 'kiss me. Hold me.'

It was what she wanted, what she'd always wanted. The desire that had always smouldered between them blazed to life, burning away her fear, lighting the night with fire.

'James,' she sighed.

Her arms rose slowly and curled around his neck, her mouth parted to the silken thrust of his tongue. James was a candle, she a moth eager for the heated embrace that offered life-giving warmth at the risk of flaming death.

She moaned softly as his hands moved over her. Her nipples swelled beneath his touch, blindly seeking his caress; her hips moved against his, beginning a *pas de deux* as old as time.

James cupped her face and kissed her, deep, passionate kisses so hot that they sent a dizzying weakness shooting through her. She fell back against the wall, taking his weight on hers, feeling the muscled power of his body against the length of her flesh.

She watched through half-closed eyes as he drew back and pulled off his jacket, then his sweater. Moonlight touched his chest with silver magic.

Her hands lifted slowly to him. He caught his breath when she put her fingertips on his skin, murmured her name when she flattened her palms against him. His skin was warm to the touch; it felt like silk that had been heated before the fire, and she made a little sound in the back of her throat when he covered her hands with his.

'Now you,' he whispered.

She looked at him and smiled unsteadily. She hesitated, gaining confidence from the night fire in his eyes, then reached for the hem of her sweater and pulled it over her head.

His mouth tightened with desire as he looked at her. She knew how she must appear, her hair dishevelled, her breasts clearly outlined beneath her silk chemise, and seeing the effect it had on James excited her. Everything that was happening between them was new to her, but the instincts of Eve were in her blood this night; she knew ways to please him, secrets that were as old as lovers and time.

She put her hands to her breasts. 'Kiss me, James,' she whispered.

He groaned and bent to her, his mouth closing lightly around her silk-covered nipple, his teeth and then his tongue teasing her through the soft fabric. Gabrielle's head fell back and she clasped his head to her, her fingers tangling in the thick hair at the nape of his neck.

'James,' she sighed.

He drew away the rest of her clothing, stripping them from her with hands that trembled as hers did, stopping when she was dressed only in the chemise and lace underpants she wore beneath. Then he caught her hands in his and brought them to his lips, kissing the palms, wetting them with his tongue.

'Take my clothes off, Gabrielle,' he said softly.

Her hands shook as she undid his belt and pulled his jeans from him, leaving him only in dark briefs that clung like skin to his narrow hips. She knelt to ease the jeans down his legs and her breath caught.

'James—your knee. Your poor knee.' It was swollen and hot to the touch, and her throat constricted. 'James,' she whispered, looking up at him, 'I'm so sorry.'

He smiled and caught her by the shoulders, lifting her to her feet.

'It's all right, love.'

It wasn't, she knew that. She had hurt him. Worse still, she'd done it trying to defend herself against him. She knew that, too. But James was kissing her again, touching her, stripping away first the chemise and then the panties, seeing her as no man ever had, and her mind blurred.

Reality skittered away, driven out by a desire that thickened her blood. The feel of James's roughened fingertips on her breasts was exquisite, a sensation like none she'd ever known before. His lips followed his hands, and, when he drew first one nipple and then the other into his mouth, she cried out.

He stepped free of his briefs and took her into his arms again. His erect flesh pressed against her and she felt the room spin away.

'James,' she said, her voice fierce with urgency, 'James...'

'Yes,' he whispered, 'yes, my love.'

They sank to the floor in a tangle of heated flesh and limbs. James pulled her into the curve of his shoulder and kissed her everywhere, from her closed eyelids to her mouth, from her throat to her breasts. His tongue dipped into her navel, and finally she felt his mouth at her thighs, then at the hidden centre of her womanhood.

She cried out as he tasted her. Tears rose in her eyes and hung on her lashes.

'James,' she sobbed, 'I want—I want...'

'Tell me,' he said. 'Tell me what you want.'

She gave a smile so radiant that it made his breath catch.

'You, James.' Her arms lifted to him and she sighed. 'You're all I've ever wanted.'

And even in the first thrust of his body, in that moment when Gabrielle left innocence behind forever, she knew it was true.

Gabrielle awoke slowly. It was very late—the dark night held within it a silence that spoke of the small hours between midnight and dawn. The sound of distant thunder rolled across the sky; a jagged bolt of lightning cast a sudden illumination into her bedroom. They had moved there hours before, when the floor became impossibly hard beneath them.

She looked at James, asleep next to her. He was lying on his side, one arm beneath her, the other thrown possessively across her body. How beautiful he was, she thought, how perfect.

'Not perfect,' he'd said with a smile when she'd whispered those words to him hours before. He'd kissed her, gently at first, then more deeply, and then he'd smiled. 'If I were perfect, I'd be able to ignore this damned knee and make love to you again.'

'James—I'm so sorry. I wish...'

'Hush.' He'd put his fingers lightly over her mouth and smiled into her eyes. 'We'll talk about it later. For now...' His smile had changed, becoming a message for her alone, and he'd rolled her on top of him. 'There's a way we can deal with this knee,' he'd said slowly. 'Let me show you.'

Warmth filled her veins. He *had* shown her, and then he'd shown her other things, other ways they could pleasure each other. Finally, James had taken her in his arms and pressed a kiss on each eyelid.

'Get some sleep, love,' he'd whispered, and before she had been able to say anything, he was asleep, his breathing shallow and steady, his skin warm against hers, and finally Gabrielle had sighed and closed her eyes, too.

Dark thoughts had writhed in her mind, monsters trying to surface from an uneasy sea, but she'd forced them all away. All that mattered now was that James hadn't been able to do whatever—whatever he'd been sent to do. She'd deal with the rest later, she'd told herself, and then sleep had claimed her.

Now, awakened by the storm that plundered the sleeping city, Gabrielle stirred uneasily.

'Later' had arrived, and she was desperate for answers.

She had given James her body and her heart. She loved him, and she regretted neither.

Was she sick? Had the past months twisted her mind?

How could she love the man sent to silence her? How could she love a killer?

She couldn't. It was impossible. Obviously, James couldn't be a killer—there had to be some mistake. A man who could be hired to take a life would have to be compassionless and brutal, and James was neither.

And yet—and yet . . .

The ring of the telephone pierced the night. The sound made Gabrielle bolt upright in bed; memories of the long vigil preceding her father's death inundated her.

'Don't answer it.' James's voice was husky with sleep, but his reflexes were quick. He caught her hand as she reached for the phone. 'Wait until I get to the kitchen extension.'

'But why? James?'

The phone shrilled again as he slipped from the bed. Gabrielle waited, her heart racing, until she heard him call her.

'Now,' he said, and she lifted the receiver.

'Hello? Who is——?'

Her eyes widened. The voice in her ear was one she hadn't heard in months, but she knew it instantly. It was Townsend, from the federal prosecutor's office, and he wasted no time on formalities.

'This is Sam Townsend, Miss Chiari. Get out of your house. Vitale's located you—he's sent a man to kill you.'

Gabrielle's mouth went dry. *James.* He was warning her against James. Oh, God.

'No.' Her answer whispered over the long-distance line. 'No,' she said more clearly, 'you're wrong. It's not true.'

The prosecutor cursed sharply. 'Don't argue, dammit. There's no time.'

'You don't understand,' she said desperately. 'He isn't like that. I know him. He wouldn't . . .'

The prosecutor's voice dripped with disgust. 'Are you blind or stupid, Miss Chiari? Are you going to protect slime like Vitale forever?'

Vitale. The fool thought she was talking about Tony Vitale. But she wasn't, she was talking about James; she was telling him that James would never hurt her, that there had been some terrible mistake.

'Miss Chiari. Get out of there, fast. Go to a neighbour. Start yelling "fire". Do something until the police get there. I'm calling them now.'

The police. James, James . . .

'No! No, don't do that. Don't involve the police. I'll talk to him. He's not what you think. I can make him change his mind. I——'

She heard a click, then another, and the line went dead. She caught the covers in her hand and drew them to her chin as James stepped into the room, wearing his jeans and shirt. Lightning tore the sky, illuminating his face.

'Get up.' His voice was as cold as his eyes.

Gabrielle could hear the racing beat of her heart. The night was warm, but she began to shiver.

Whatever James was, he wasn't a killer.

She believed that, she had to go on believing it. There was some rational explanation for what was happening.

'I'm not afraid, James,' she said. But her voice quavered and she had to inhale deeply before she could go on. 'Do you hear me? The prosecutor and his agents are fools—they always were. They're——'

James moved slowly to the side of the bed. 'Get up,' he said softly, 'and get dressed.'

'James, listen to me. I——'

'Gabrielle.' His voice was sharp. 'Do as I tell you. Do it now.'

Thunder roared through the Quarter like a runaway train while lightning lit the room again, bathing everything in an eerie glow.

Gabrielle's heart almost stopped beating as she looked at James.

His face was taut with tension. He had changed back into the stranger she'd met a lifetime ago.

CHAPTER TEN

GABRIELLE moved swiftly, stumbling from the bed, pulling on her discarded clothing, her eyes never leaving his. Her body was an automaton that didn't need to think about buttons and zippers, her mind a computer chasing down a thousand paths simultaneously.

James wouldn't hurt her. He couldn't.

But there he was, watching her coldly, hurrying her with muttered oaths, as if what they'd shared this night had been a fabrication of her imagination.

'Hurry, dammit.'

One of her shoes lay beside the bed. She picked it up, then began searching for the other.

'Gabrielle. Did you hear what I said?'

She looked at him. 'I can't find my other shoe.'

He slapped the shoe from her hand and it clattered to the floor.

'Forget the damned shoes. You won't need them.'

'James. Listen to me. Whatever you think you have to do——'

'Get over here.' He caught her by the shoulder, his fingers biting into her flesh, and began pulling her across the room with him. 'Now move,' he said, his voice curt with tension.

'James.' She stumbled as he drew her into the dark hall. Fear filled her mouth with cotton. 'James,' she said again, 'don't. I beg you.'

'Do you hear me? Move, Gabrielle. Move.'

The stairs loomed ahead, dark and foreboding.

'You have to listen to me,' she said. 'You don't have to do this, James. You can't. You...'

137

He wasn't listening. He was propelling her down the steps, then along the hall. The storm had abated, and the sudden quiet was menacing.

'James,' she said, her voice low and desperate, 'please. Let me talk to you.'

'We're done talking. It's over, Gabrielle. Finished. Tonight ends it.'

A sob burst from her throat. 'No. God, no. Don't you have any feelings? I know you don't want to do this, James, I——'

'I never did. Hell, I knew it was a mistake. But there was no one else, nobody who would...' He cursed softly. 'Never mind that now,' he said, pushing open the door to the bedroom he'd used the night before. 'Just get in there,' he said, and he shoved her into the dark.

What was he telling her? Was he saying he'd come into her life by design, so he could gain her trust and then—and then...?

They faced each other in a silence broken only by the ragged sounds of their breathing. A weak moon played hide and seek with the clouds, splashing the room with pale, broken light. James's eyes were as cold as she'd ever seen them.

It was clear now. Everything that had happened between them—the laughter, the easy chatter, the sweet hours spent in his arms—all of it had been part of a plan that led to this one moment. She could only speculate why he hadn't let the speeding truck do the job for him the morning they'd met.

Maybe he'd been afraid it wouldn't be as final as he wanted it to be.

Maybe he enjoyed his work too much.

The obscenity of it all rose in her throat, gagging her with nausea. What kind of man found pleasure in taking a woman from passion to death, all in one night?

Gabrielle began to tremble. She felt soiled. Had she ever loved James? Had she ever thought that this man with ice in his veins cared for her?

She had been caught in an illusion of her own making, and now reality had returned. With a self-loathing fuelled by her hatred of the man standing before her, rage exploded inside her. She flew at him, her hand clawing across his face.

James gasped and took a step back. He looked stunned, she thought with bitter satisfaction. What had he expected? Was she supposed to walk to her death in the same trance she'd been in since they'd met?

She struck out at him again, but this time he caught her by the wrist. 'Gabrielle, goddammit,' he said, pulling her arm up, twisting it behind her back so that she cried out. 'Are you crazy?'

No, she thought. Maybe she had been, but not now.

'Let go of me, damn you!'

He pulled her arm higher. Pain shot from her wrist to her shoulder.

'You heard what Townsend said. Vitale——'

'Did you think I'd make it easy for you?' She was panting now, her hair fallen over her face in disarray, and she tossed it back. 'Well, I'm not. I'm not going to just...'

He hauled her against him, pinning her arms to her side with his embrace. She could feel the hard, angry beat of his heart. His jaw jutted forward as he pushed his face to hers.

'What will it take to make you listen to reason? I don't care what kind of sugar-daddy Vitale's been to you. He wants you dead tonight.'

Gabrielle twisted wildly against him. 'What kind of man are you, James? How could you agree to do this?'

He laughed. 'A damn good question, baby. It was my idea. Can you believe that? I volunteered.'

'Volunteered?' she whispered.

'I told Townsend I'd keep you alive, and I will—even if you're too pig-headed to believe your "uncle" has decided to pull the plug.'

Gabrielle went still in his arms. *I told Townsend I'd keep you alive* . . .

Townsend, the federal prosecutor?

'Do you hear me, Gabrielle?'

I told Townsend I'd keep you alive, and I will . . .

James wasn't a criminal, he'd told Townsend he'd keep her alive.

Who was he, then?

Nothing made sense, she thought, staring at him. His face was carved in steel, his eyes unreadable.

'Are you going to behave?' he asked. She swallowed, then nodded. His hands fell away from her and he stepped back. 'Stay here, be quiet as a mouse. Whatever happens, don't leave this room.'

'James. You have to tell me who——'

'Do you hear me? I don't give a damn if the house starts to fall down around your ears, Gabrielle. You don't open that door once it closes after me. Have you got it?'

She looked from him to the dark hallway. Fear turned her blood to water as the reality of what was happening settled on her. Someone was coming to her, someone who wanted to kill her. And James was going to stop him, he was going out there to face a killer, he was going to risk his life.

'No.' Her voice sounded unnaturally loud. 'James, don't. Please.'

There was a sound from the rear of the house, tinkling glass and then a soft thud. Gabrielle's eyes grew wide; she opened her mouth but James shook his head.

He put his lips against her ear. 'Remember,' he breathed, 'quiet as a mouse.'

'Where are you——?'

He put his hand over her mouth. 'Later,' he whispered.

She sighed his name against his skin. He made a sound in the back of his throat and then he pulled her to him. His mouth fell on hers with a bruising passion—she tasted the salt tang of blood against her tongue, felt the hard lines of his body against hers, and then he was gone.

She stared at the door as it closed after him. Stay here, he'd said, but how could she, when somewhere in the darkness a killer waited?

A killer. Tony Vitale had sent someone to end her life. Gabrielle sank on the edge of the bed and wrapped her arms around herself. Scenes from her life flashed before her. Her father, kind and loving. 'Uncle' Tony, generous to a fault. One a chauffeur, the other a union official—so she'd believed.

Had they been something different? Had it all been a sham?

And the past days, with James. Had all that been a lie, too? She couldn't think that. No. No!

She sprang up, every nerve-end alert, as she heard the sounds of scuffling in the hall. Flesh thudded against flesh; someone grunted in pain. Gabrielle ran across the room and leaned against the closed door, hands spread against the wood, feeling the shuddering blows as if they were being struck against her own body.

James's name was a silent cry on her lips. Stay here, he'd said, but she couldn't. She had to know what was happening in the hall. Suppose he needed her help? Suppose...?

Something thudded heavily against the door, then slid to the floor.

Silence fell over the house.

Gabrielle began to pant. The air was being drawn from her lungs. Her heart stopped, then began again, galloping like a runaway horse.

She stepped back, knuckles to her mouth, as the door opened and a man stepped into the room. He was tall, broad of shoulder...

'James!'

She sobbed his name aloud and rushed towards him. 'Are you all right? I thought—I was afraid...'

The lights came one, pushing away the darkness. Gabrielle stared at him in horror.

He looked the same, yet different. His shirt was torn, his face bloodied, but that wasn't what made the change. It was something else, a glittering coldness in his eyes, perhaps, or the way he was looking at her.

'You're hurt,' she said.

He leaned against the wall and took a deep breath. 'I'm fine.'

'Your face—it's bleeding.'

He touched his hand to his cheek. His fingers came away crimson. He stared at them blindly, then shrugged and wiped his hand on his shirt. 'It's nothing. A couple of stitches pulled open, that's all.' He looked at her again, then shouldered past her to the bed and sank down on it. 'The police are on their way.'

She nodded. There were sirens slashing the night—she had not really heard them until he mentioned it, but now she realised she'd been listening to their wail in the distance for the past few seconds.

'It took them long enough,' she said slowly, her eyes searching his face.

James leaned back against the headboard. 'You know the old saying.' He gave her a quick smile. 'There's never a cop around when you want one.'

Gabrielle looked into the hall. A man was lying sprawled on the floor. He was enormous. A shudder went through her when she saw the knife lying beside him.

'Is he...? Did you...?'

James shook his head. 'No.' His voice was hoarse with fatigue, and he put his hand to his face, wincing as he touched his cheek. 'I didn't have to. I hit him with a cast-iron skillet. He'll have one hell of a headache, but he'll live.' His hands fell to his lap and he looked at her.

'Maybe you want to go take a look at him. He might be someone you know.'

Her face paled. 'What are you talking about?'

'Come on, it's not hard to figure. I doubt if Vitale could get outside talent to do this job. Since he was indicted, nobody wants to know him.' He jerked his head towards the hall, but his eyes didn't leave hers. 'That guy may turn out to be an old friend.'

Gabrielle swallowed. 'I don't think that's very funny,' she said. Her voice quavered, and she swallowed again. 'If it's true, if Vitale sent him . . .'

He laughed. 'If? If? What the hell does it take to convince you, lady?'

Didn't he understand? She was beginning to know the truth—perhaps she'd always known it, deep in her heart.

But admitting it to herself was painful. Vitale had been the only family she'd known. And her father—the pain of accepting the truth about him was more than she could bear.

'James,' she said, holding her hand out to him, 'try to see it through my eyes. Please.'

His voice was flat. 'That's just what I'm doing, Gabrielle. Seeing it through your eyes, hearing it through your words . . .'

'What do you mean?'

'What was all that stuff on the phone with Townsend?'

'What stuff? I don't——'

His hand cut through the air in impatience. 'Come on, don't play coy. I heard you, remember?' His voice mimicked hers cruelly. ' "He isn't like that. I know him." ' His mouth twisted. 'How long are you going to go on kidding yourself?'

Was that why he was so angry? The frantic conversation with the federal prosecutor came back to her in bits and pieces; she remembered the things she'd said, and she knew how they might have sounded, but she'd been talking about James, not Vitale; she'd said those things when she still thought James was...

How could she tell him that? How could she tell him she'd thought he'd been sent to kill her?

'It's—it's hard to explain,' she said slowly.

James's eyes bored into hers. 'Try.'

She opened her mouth, then shut it. She barely understood it herself. She had fallen in love with him, then feared him, but her doubts about him had fallen away in his arms. She had known James could not be evil.

And then the middle-of-the-night call had come from Townsend. It had been disorientating. There'd been no time to think or reason, there'd only been time to react.

'I'm waiting,' James said coldly. 'Why don't you just try telling me the truth?' A muscle bunched in his jaw. 'Or is that beyond you?'

Gabrielle's chin lifted. What right had he to talk to her like this? She'd done nothing to warrant it except trust him, even in the face of the warning she'd thought Townsend had been trying to give her.

'If you want to talk about "truth",' she said softly, her eyes on his, 'we ought to talk about you, don't you think?'

James rose to his feet. 'My turn, hmm?' The muscle in his jaw jumped again. 'All right. But you're not going to like it.'

Her heart softened. 'You just saved my life,' she said. 'Nothing you could say can diminish that.'

He stared at her for a moment, then stuffed his hands into his pockets and walked across the room. At the door, he turned and faced her.

'My name is James Forrester and I live in Washington. That much you already know.'

She waited for him to speak again, but he remained silent, and finally she ran her tongue lightly over her dry lips.

'We didn't meet by accident, did we?'

James bent his head, his eyes refusing to meet hers. 'No,' he said after a moment. 'I'd been in New Orleans for weeks, watching you. You'd walked away from protective custody, but I—we knew you wouldn't be safe. I—we decided someone had to make sure nothing happened to you.'

She nodded. She'd figured as much by now. Was he an agent? A police officer, perhaps, from up north? Whatever he was, she could accept it. She loved him.

'Are you with the police department?'

James shook his head. 'No.'

'Then you're an investigator.'

He shook his head again. 'I'm an attorney.' His jaw shot forward belligerently. 'A federal attorney.' There was a silence, and then he cleared his throat. 'I work in Townsend's office.'

The admission stunned her. 'You work in...' She put her hand to her mouth. 'Were you—were you involved in—in...?'

He nodded. 'Yes.' He took a deep breath. 'You might as well know the worst. I'm the guy who put together the dossier on your old man.'

'No.' Her whisper echoed in the room.

'Yes.' His voice was flat. 'And then I came up with the idea of putting the screws on you after he got sick.'

'No,' she said again, her eyes widening in horror. Not James. It couldn't have been James. Her eyes lifted to his. 'Then why—if you're an attorney, why did you come to New Orleans? Why did they send you?'

'They didn't. I told you, I volunteered.' His mouth twisted. 'There was no other way. The cops had no legal right to hold you. Neither did my office. So I took a leave of absence...'

The horror of it was beginning to seep through. James was responsible for the web that had ensnared her, not Townsend. It had been James all along.

She held up her hands. 'I don't want to hear any more,' she whispered. 'Please.'

'Damn you, Gabrielle!' He reached out and caught her by the wrists, his fingers clamping hard on the fragile bones. 'I was only doing my job. You were a name in a file, a snapshot clipped to a fact sheet.' He moved towards her, his face drawn with anguish. 'I didn't plan on falling in love with you, but I did. It was why I came after you. I told myself it was because I was responsible, but it was more than that...'

James was saying things, she knew that, but she wasn't really listening. All she could think of was how she'd hated Townsend and now...

'You did this,' she said, 'not Townsend. It was you all the time.'

His arms closed around her. 'Gabrielle.' His voice was urgent. 'We'll put all of this behind us.' She shook her head and he cursed softly. 'Look at me, dammit!'

Her head rose slowly and she looked into his eyes. This was the man who had made her see the truth about her father, this was the man who'd destroyed her life—the man she'd fallen in love with.

'Gabrielle. We can forget everything. You and Vitale. Me and Townsend...'

Forget. Could she? Face the past squarely, James had said, so you can put it behind you.

They'd done that tonight, but somehow it wasn't behind them. It had only deepened the uncertainty that lay ahead.

'I—I don't know if I can,' she whispered, her voice breaking.

Brakes squealed outside; flashing lights lit the house with an eerie glow, and suddenly there was a banging at the door.

'Police!'

James cupped her face in his hands. 'Gabrielle,' he said in a fierce whisper, and then he kissed her. When he drew back, he looked deep into her eyes. 'I love you,' he said. 'Do you understand?'

There was a heavy blow on the front door, the sound of splintering wood, and then the house was filled with policemen.

'Gabrielle?'

James was still watching her, waiting for her to answer, and suddenly she knew he was right.

Her father had believed in some fierce, time-worn code she didn't understand. Her love for him would never change, but that part of her life was over.

The future lay ahead, and it was the future that mattered. James loved her, and nothing else was important.

Tears of happiness rose in her eyes. 'James,' she whispered.

'Are you people OK?'

James and Gabrielle fell apart. A man in plain clothes, a gold and enamel badge pinned to his jacket, stood beside them, and a sea of blue uniforms stretched away behind him.

James nodded. 'We're fine, Officer. I'm James Forrester. This is Gabrielle Chiari. And that man in the hall...'

The detective nodded. 'Yeah, yeah, I've been on the horn with Washington.' He looked from Gabrielle to James. 'You're gonna have to come to the station, Forrester. We'll need a statement.'

James nodded. 'Fine. But Miss Chiari——'

'She stays here. Don't worry, I already got the word from Washington. Two of my people will stay with her.'

James looked at her and she smiled tremulously. What he wanted to hear, what she wanted to tell him, couldn't be said in a room filled with strangers.

'I'll be fine,' she said.

He touched her cheek, and then he was gone.

* * *

She awoke groggily, every muscle stiff and aching. The phone was ringing; she groaned as she uncurled from the living-room couch and made her way through the still-dark house to the kitchen.

What time was it, anyway? she thought, pushing her hand through her hair. She must have dozed off while she was reading. James wasn't back yet—she wouldn't sleep soundly until she was safe in his arms. Not that she was in any danger: there was a policeman outside the front door, another at the back.

But she had never, in all her life, felt as secure and as loved as she had with James beside her. And he would be beside her forever, she thought with a little smile; he loved her and she loved him. She would tell him that the moment she saw him. She would tell him that now.

'James?' she whispered, smiling into the phone as she put it to her ear.

'Hello, Gabriella.'

She froze, the smile tumbling from her lips. *Gabriella.* No one had ever called her that except—except...

'Gabriella.' Tony Vitale's voice wheezed softly. She closed her eyes, picturing him chewing on one of the black cigars he favoured. 'Aren't you going to say hello to Uncle Tony?'

'What—what do you——?' She stopped, drew a shaky breath, then began again. 'Why are you calling me?'

He laughed. 'Why shouldn't an uncle say hello to his favourite niece, Gabriella?'

Bile rose in her throat. 'You—you're not my uncle,' she said. 'And you—you tried to—you sent someone to...'

'You see, *cara mia*? You see what's happened? Now you believe the terrible things you are told about me, hmm? That liar, Forrester...'

Gabrielle sank into a chair. 'James isn't a liar,' she whispered, her voice shaking. 'You are. You—you're everything they said you were. You——'

'Gabriella.' The husky voice was harsh. 'I have a proposition to make you. Are you listening?'

'A proposition?'

'Yes. What your lawyer friend would call a quid pro quo.'

James. He kept referring to James. What did he know about him?

'I regret what almost happened tonight, Gabriella.' Vitale's voice dropped to a wheezing whisper. 'It was an unfortunate mistake.'

She sprang to her feet. 'Do you know what I'm going to do?' she said. 'I'm going to come back to New York. I'm going to testify. I——'

Vitale laughed. 'Yes, *cara mia*, you will come back. But not to testify.' He paused, and she could almost see the smile moving across his sallow face. 'You will come back and marry me, Gabriella.'

Hysterical laughter burst from her throat. 'I'll what? Marry you? I'd sooner be dead. I——'

'What of your precious Mr Forrester, Gabriella? Would you sooner *he* be dead?'

Her heart stopped beating. 'What?'

Vitale's voice was cold. 'You will return to New York. You will wear my furs, my jewels, you will face the world as my wife. And you will convince everyone that you do it proudly.'

'You're insane. You——'

'The fool the police arrested bungled his job, Gabriella. Another incident would be far too obvious. The risk would be too great.' His voice became a purr. 'If your performance pleases me, I will let Forrester live. Otherwise...'

Gabrielle's legs turned to jelly. 'Dear God,' she whispered. 'What have you done to him? Please...'

Vitale laughed. The laughter became a wheeze, and he coughed heavily before he spoke again. 'Nothing—but things *could* happen. A mechanism might be placed under the hood of his car. Perhaps an accident on his way to the office. A sudden encounter on a crowded street...'

Gabrielle moaned softly. 'You wouldn't. I beg you...'

'The policeman at your front door will be missing from his post for the next five minutes,' Vitale said coldly. 'A taxi will pull up outside your house. It will take you to the airport. There will be a ticket to New York waiting at the United Airlines counter.' He paused. 'If you care for your Mr Forrester, you will collect your ticket and get on that flight.'

The phone went dead in her hands. Gabrielle sat staring at it, then slowly hung up.

Surely, this was all a bad dream.

Her eyes skimmed across the cast-iron skillets neatly stacked beside the stove.

One was missing. The police had taken it with them as evidence, along with the knife that had been meant for her.

Slowly, as if she had aged years in the past moments, Gabrielle got to her feet and started towards the front door.

CHAPTER ELEVEN

THE Vitale house dated from the turn of the century. Large, graceless, with endless dark rooms opening on to even darker halls, the house was Victorian in concept, but completely lacking in any of the period's charm or grace. Everything about it was sombre and oppressive, from the wainscoted walls to the oversized furniture.

Gabrielle had avoided the house all her life, entering it only when she had had no choice. As a child, she'd clung to her father's hand whenever they stepped over the threshold. She remembered worrying that something terrible lurked in the shadowy corners of the entrance hall, something that would make the trolls and witches who lived in her book of Grimm's *Fairy Tales* pale in comparison. As she'd grown older, of course, she'd learned there was nothing supernatural to fear in the Vitale house.

There had been only 'Uncle' Tony. And it had taken a lifetime, and what had happened on a hot night in New Orleans three months ago, to make her face the truth, which was that 'Uncle' Tony was far more evil than any of the ghouls or goblins that lived in the pages of the old fairy-stories.

Now, on this sweet-smelling June day, as she sat in the window-seat of her room on the third floor of the old house, Gabrielle wondered how she could have been so blind to the truth. Tony Vitale was a crook—there was no kinder way to phrase it. And she—she was his prisoner.

She sighed as she watched the gardener weeding the roses. She was too old to believe in fairy-tales any more, but she knew how Rapunzel must have felt, locked in the tower with no hope of rescue. No matter how luxurious the furnishings, there was nothing more terrible than to know you were someone's captive, unless it was to know you would remain so for the rest of your life.

She hadn't wanted to believe any of it, at first. After the phone had gone dead in her hands that night in New Orleans, she'd told herself the conversation with Vitale couldn't have really taken place. Things like that didn't happen in the real world, she'd thought, making her way slowly to the front door.

Carefully, she'd opened the wrought-iron grille and peered out. The policeman left to guard her had been standing a few feet from the carriage house, his arms folded across his chest, and she'd breathed a relieved sigh—until suddenly he'd pushed back his sleeve, glanced at his watch, and then cast a furtive glance to the side. Seconds later, he'd stepped into the shadows in the courtyard, vanishing as neatly as a rabbit down a hole. And then a taxi had glided silently to the kerb, its headlights peering myopically into the wispy fog, and a terror greater than any she'd ever known had swarmed through Gabrielle's body.

The truth, so long denied, had finally become irrefutable. Tony Vitale—'Uncle' Tony—had tried to have her killed tonight, but the attempt had failed.

James was his next target.

She'd spun on her heel towards the telephone. She'd call James at the police station, tell him . . .

Tell him what? That Vitale had targeted him for death? She knew how James would react to that. The threat would enrage him, but it certainly wouldn't make him cautious. That wasn't the kind of man he was. Besides, Vitale himself had told her he wouldn't do anything overt. How could anyone protect James from an 'accident'? A speeding car, a bomb, a package in the mail—

there were endless ways to do the job, and she probably didn't even know half of them.

Wrapped in the trappings of respectability, Vitale was a powerful figure. His patronage gave him access into high places; he could do anything he wanted. Anything.

He could have James killed, and no one could stop him.

She had moved like a robot, stepping out into the night, slipping out of the gate and into the waiting taxi. Her ticket had been waiting at the airport, just as Vitale had promised, and she had boarded the plane without looking back, afraid that if she did she would somehow see James's face and know she couldn't leave him, no matter what.

The flight to New York had seemed to take forever, but finally it had ended. She had stepped from the plane and into the heavy arms of Tony Vitale.

'Don't,' she'd said, struggling to free herself, but Vitale had only drawn her closer to him. The mingled scents of cigar smoke and cologne had made her gag.

'Smile for the birdie, Gabriella,' Vitale had whispered, his cheek rasping against hers.

Flashbulbs had gone off in her eyes. Blinking, she'd stared into a dozen cameras and she'd realised they were surrounded by reporters and photographers.

'My insurance policy, *cara mia*,' Vitale had said with a laugh, curving his arm around her waist as he led her through the terminal and to his waiting limousine. 'By tomorrow morning, your boyfriend won't be able to pick up a newspaper without seeing a photograph of our tender reconciliation.'

Tears had streamed down her face as Vitale handed her into the car. 'Why?' she'd whispered, staring at the man she'd once felt such affection for as he climbed heavily in beside her. 'Why are you doing this?'

Vitale's thick brows had drawn together. 'Are you such a fool, Gabriella? I can't allow you to testify against me. Don't you understand?'

'A wife can testify against her husband,' Gabriella had said quickly. 'I know that. I——'

He'd waved his hand in dismissal. 'Never mind "can",' he'd said. 'What matters is that she can't be forced to testify.' An oily smile had crept over his face. 'And no one will be able to force you, will they, *cara*? Not when the stakes are so high, and your precious Mr Forrester's life hangs in the balance.'

Gabrielle had taken a deep breath. 'Please,' she'd said desperately, 'you have to listen to me. I don't know anything.'

'You do, *cara*. You know enough to corroborate Frank Lorenzo's testimony.'

She'd looked at him blankly. 'Frank? The man who works for you?'

He'd nodded as he settled back in the car and pulled a long, black cigar from the breast pocket of his silk suit.

'Yes.' Vitale had chewed off the end of the cigar and spat it on to the carpeted floor. 'That's right.'

'Is that the man you were on the phone with that time? But I told the prosecutor, I only heard a few meaningless words...'

Vitale had smiled, almost sadly. 'Tell me what you heard, Gabriella.'

'I heard—I heard you say—you said, "Riley refuses to come around, Frank. I want him taken care of tonight."'

Her eyes had met his. Suddenly, the simple words seemed to take on a darker meaning than they ever had before.

Vitale had put his hand over hers, clasping it tightly when she tried to pull free.

'Yes. That's right, *cara*. I was talking to Frank Lorenzo. And that night, Riley was killed. Someone put a gun to his head and...'

Gabrielle had shaken her head. 'No,' she'd said sharply. 'I don't want to hear.'

She'd cried out as Vitale's hand almost crushed hers. 'You already did,' he'd said with deadly calm. 'You heard me give the order for his death. The federal authorities have Frank in custody—they have for months—and they've offered him immunity if he'll testify against me.'

Gabrielle had stared at him. 'Then he's the one, not me. Not——'

Vitale's smile had become a snarl. 'Are you stupid, Gabriella? I told you, they need your testimony to corroborate his.' He had stared at her for a moment and then, gradually, his smile had returned and the pressure on her hand had eased. 'But you're not going to do that, are you, *cara*? You're going to be the good girl your dear father raised you to be. You're going to be a comfort in my old age.'

'Mr Vitale. I...'

Vitale had laughed. 'Such formality, *cara*. But of course, my future bride can't call me "Uncle" Tony, can she?'

'Please. Tell me what you want with me. My promise of silence? You have that, I swear. I won't tell anyone what I heard. I...'

It had been as if she hadn't spoken. Vitale had smiled broadly, and for a moment he'd looked as innocent and benign as he had years before, when she'd sat on his knee and laughed at his jokes.

'Your father and I were of the old country. We understood each other, Gabriella—I trusted him with my life.'

Her heart had turned over. 'No,' she'd whispered, 'not my father. He couldn't have known what you were. He...'

Vitale had shrugged her words away. 'He was my bodyguard and a good friend. And he knew how I felt about you, *cara*.' He'd smiled that oily smile that made her skin crawl. 'He hoped you would come to feel the same way about me, but things don't always work out as we would wish, do they?'

She'd stared at him. It was impossible. Her father wouldn't have wanted her to—to...

'No,' she'd whispered again. 'It's a lie. He wouldn't have. He...'

Vitale had sighed. 'He wanted you to live a safe, secure life, Gabriella—the kind of life I can provide.'

Gabrielle had looked at the man beside her and suddenly a terrible fear had swept through her.

'No,' she'd said, reaching for the door-handle, 'I won't. You can't force me.'

Vitale hadn't even moved. The doors locks were automatic; she should have remembered that from the times her father had taken her for rides in this very same limousine. She was trapped as surely as if she were caged.

'I will honour your father's memory by treating you with courtesy,' he'd said, breathing out a cloud of cigar smoke that hung in the car like a pall. 'My housekeeper will chaperon us until our wedding arrangements are completed.'

Gabrielle had shaken her head wildly. 'I won't do it. You're a—a killer. You...'

Something cold and frightening had flared in Vitale's eyes. His hand had closed around hers again and she'd moaned with pain.

'You will never say such things again, *cara*, do you hear me? You will treat me with respect.' And then he'd tugged her to him; the scent of his cologne had surrounded her just before he'd pressed his damp mouth to hers. She'd sat still as stone, trembling in his unwanted embrace, until finally he'd drawn back and looked into her eyes. 'And if you decide to change your mind, Gabriella, I suggest you think of Mr Forrester and remember that his life is in your lovely hands.'

Three months had passed since then, three months of living locked within this ugly house except when Vitale chose to take her out of it. He seemed to get a special pleasure out of exhibiting her in public, as if she were a prize specimen he'd collected on a hunting trip. The tabloids recorded her every move, along with the gossip magazines, and their attention pleased Vitale.

'Smile for the birdie' became his favourite expression whenever he saw a camera.

After a while, she suspected he arranged for the reporters and photographers always to be on hand when she stepped out the door. She knew the reason: he was drawing her ever more deeply into his web, branding her so firmly as his that she would never be able to escape, even if she were foolish enough to try.

Not that she would. James's life hung in her hands, Vitale had said, and Gabrielle knew it was the truth. Vitale, now that she allowed herself to see him as he really was, was a ruthless thug. She had no doubt that he would kill James if she thwarted him.

As for the rest—it hurt to admit that her father had known what Vitale was, had in some way been part of Vitale's criminal empire, but she had to accept the past. 'Face it squarely,' James had said, 'and then you can put it behind you,' and that was what she was doing. Her father's connection to Vitale didn't change the fact that he'd been a loving father to her.

But there was a part of the past she didn't want to forget, that she would never forget, and that was James and how much she loved him.

She dreamed of him at night, lying in the huge four-poster bed in her room, restless against the satin sheets hand-embroidered with her initials. She thought of him when the limousine rolled silently along the city streets and she saw lovers walking arm in arm on the pavement.

James, her heart would sigh silently, James.

Where was he? What was he doing? Did he hate her? She knew he must; Vitale had explained to the Press that she had come back to him unexpectedly—'A joyous reunion' was how one tabloid had described it—after a foolish misunderstanding. Thanks to his sly use of the media, a myth was growing up around her.

It was as if America had fallen in love with someone a little soiled and sordid. It wasn't a new phenomenon: there'd always been a place in the public heart for women of tarnished virtue.

A tabloid dubbed Gabrielle 'The Silent Princess' and other papers picked up the designation, describing in gushing terms her cool beauty and her refusal to respond to questions, dwelling with relish on the arrangements for the forthcoming marriage between her and Vitale. Her photos appeared in the gossip columns with regularity, showing her wrapped in sable or mink, jewels gleaming at her ears and throat, Vitale's obscenely large diamond on her finger.

Gabrielle had difficulty recognising herself in the pictures. She'd lost weight, and the woman the cameras captured was a hollow-cheeked stranger designed by Vitale. Her long hair was caught in a demure chignon, her make-up was lavish and impeccable as he demanded. Only her eyes were familiar. She wondered if only she could see the terrible sadness in them.

She started at the sound of a heavy-knuckled knock at the door. She knew it was Vitale. But he'd said a meeting would keep him late at the office, and she had looked forward to the extra time without him.

'Gabriella?' The door opened and he stepped into the room, smiling as he saw her. 'Ah, *cara*, there you are.'

He sounded jovial, the charming husband returned from his humdrum nine-to-five job, delighted to find his wife at home.

But the picture was warped. His 'job' was hardly the nine to five kind. They were not yet married. And where else would she be, when he kept her a virtual prisoner in his home?

Gabrielle slipped from the window-seat and faced him. 'Of course I'm here,' she said coldly. 'You've given my gaolers orders that I not leave this house without you.'

Vitale laughed. 'Such nonsense. I'm concerned for your welfare, *cara*. A man in my position has many enemies, you know that.'

A terrible weariness gripped her. They had been through all this a dozen times before, she at first demanding freedom of movement, then pleading for it. But he was never going to allow her any. She knew that, just as she knew there was no way out of this nightmare she was living, and she was suddenly tired. So tired.

She crossed the room and sat down at her dressing-table. It was, Vitale had told her proudly, Louis XIV—or had he said Louis XV? Not that it mattered. She hated it; it was as elaborate and overblown as everything else in the velvet cage that was her bedroom.

'What do you want?' she asked, picking up a comb and running it through her hair. The comb was made of tortoiseshell, trimmed in eighteen-carat gold set with tiny sprays of diamonds, and not a day passed but that she thought about snapping it in half. 'You said you would be late today.'

Vitale walked up behind her. She flinched as his meaty hands settled on her shoulders and he smiled at her in the mirror.

'Is that the warmest greeting you can manage for your fiancé, Gabriella?' His hands slipped to her throat and he tipped her head up, watching her reflection in the mirror. 'Surely you can think of something more cordial?'

A sour taste filled her mouth. She swallowed, then swallowed again. Vitale had kept to his promise so far: he hadn't touched her intimately, or even tried to. But she felt his eyes on her all the time, moving over her body like snails, leaving slime wherever they touched.

She had learned that the best defence was to remain silent in the face of his taunts. But logic often gave way to the need to strike out. Her verbal blows were weak, but sometimes they struck home. Such moments were worth any risk.

'You aren't my fiancé,' she said, staring back at him. 'You're a murderer and a blackmailer, and I despise you.'

She cried out as his hands closed around her throat. 'Watch that mouth of yours, *cara*.' His voice was like granite, and her heart leaped as she felt the distinct pressure of his thumbs against her windpipe.

She looked at him steadily. 'Go on,' she said softly. 'You'd be doing me a favour.'

Their eyes held, and then Vitale laughed and his hands fell to her shoulders again.

'Why should we quarrel, *cara*? You know better than to speak your poison outside this house.' He looked at her, the expression on his face suddenly sly. 'Have you read the paper today?'

She shook her head wearily. 'No. Why? Is there something in the columns about the jewels you bought yesterday? I don't want them. I told you...'

He smiled. 'You should keep up with the news, Gabriella. There's an item about your Mr Forrester.'

Her heart tumbled. She knew what would happen if she expressed too much interest; it had happened before, just after she'd come here. Vitale had dropped a hint about James and how he'd reacted to learning she'd fled to New York, and when she'd begged him to tell her more Vitale had laughed and walked away.

Sound casual, she told herself, but when she spoke she could hear the tension in her whispered words.

'About James?'

He nodded. 'Yes. He's left Washington,' he said, watching her reflection. 'He quit the prosecutor's office.'

He waited, and then he smiled. 'I'll bet you can't imagine where he's living now.'

She stared at him, praying he couldn't hear the beat of her heart. 'No,' she said finally. 'Where?'

Vitale smiled like a shark, all teeth and no warmth. 'New York. Isn't it amazing what a small world we live in, Gabriella?'

James. James was here, in the same city.

Gabrielle swallowed drily. 'Yes,' she whispered, 'it is.'

'Do you want to know more?' He laughed. 'Then again, it's not very interesting, *cara*. I don't want to bore you.'

Oh, God. He was playing with her. He was tossing out the bait, and if she leaped too quickly he'd reel in his line and that would be the end of it.

'Do as you wish,' she said carefully, even though she wanted to leap from the chair and claw at his face.

Vitale laughed again. She felt breathless, thinking at first she'd passed the test. But she hadn't. When he spoke, she knew he'd tricked her.

'Good,' he said with a smile. 'Then we won't waste time talking about things of no importance.' He bent and put his lips to her hair, and she shuddered. He stiffened, then sought her eyes in the mirror again. 'In two weeks' time you'll be mine, *cara mia*,' he whispered. 'You will not shudder in my arms. Not if you wish your Mr Forrester to remain healthy.'

She felt a cold hand seize her heart. 'You promised,' she whispered. 'You said if I married you...'

'And now I'm adding a requirement.' His voice was as cold as his eyes were hot. 'I shall expect a woman in my bed, not a martyr. Is that clear?' Gabrielle nodded and Vitale smiled. 'Good.' His hands slid from her and he stepped back. 'We're going to the opera,' he said. 'Dinner first, at the place in the Village. Wear the white dress from Bendel's and the rubies. I'll see you downstairs in an hour.'

She nodded, sitting stiffly and watching in the mirror until he'd left the room, and then she slumped forward and buried her face in her hands.

What had he been about to tell her about James? Any little bit of news would have been wonderful: to someone dying of thirst, even a raindrop was welcome.

And Gabrielle was dying.

She was dying of sorrow.

'Smile, Gabriella.' Vitale's voice hissed in her ear. 'This is not a sad opera—looking at you, one would think this was the last act in *Camille*.'

Gabrielle straightened in the box-seat and consciously rearranged the expression on her face. She hadn't been paying attention to what was happening on stage—opera had never been among her favourite things, and tonight James's teasing words kept coming back to her.

'I think whoever invented opera did it just to confuse good music and bad theatre.'

She remembered smiling when he'd said that to her, laughing at his teasing words, and then moments later falling breathlessly into his arms while he kissed her.

Tears rose in her eyes. How he must hate her! She could imagine him that night in New Orleans, coming back to the carriage house and finding her gone, imagine how he'd felt when he'd seen those pictures of her in the papers the very next day. What had he thought when he'd seen her in Vitale's arms, their lips pressed together? What had he thought when he'd read about their wedding plans?

'Gabriella!'

She looked up, blinking back the tears. Vitale was scowling at her.

'Yes? What is it?'

His eyes moved over her face and he grimaced. 'You look cheap,' he said hoarsely. 'Your eyes are smudged. Go fix them.'

She nodded dumbly and rose to her feet. Ten minutes in the ladies' room was like time off for good behaviour. Neither Vitale nor his omnipresent bodyguards could follow her there, but one of them always escorted her to the door and waited outside.

Oh, God! She almost stumbled as she stepped into the corridor. For an instant, she felt as if she'd awakened into one of her dreams. James was here, he was walking towards her, dark and handsome in a dinner-jacket.

But it was a nightmare, not a dream. There was a woman with him, a stunning redhead. His arm was draped lightly around her shoulders and he was looking down at her and laughing at something she'd just said. The woman was smiling, watching him through shining eyes, and Gabrielle felt a sudden, irrational hatred for her begin to grow within her heart.

Still, James was all that mattered. She could no more stop herself from calling out his name than she could change the love she would always feel for him.

'James.'

It was the faintest whisper. She took a step forward. Beside her, her burly escort muttered something, but she ignored him.

'James?'

Her voice was still soft, but this time her whisper seemed to echo across the corridor, growing louder and louder, and James paused, the smile fading from his face. He looked up, and their eyes met.

'Gabrielle.'

His voice was harsh. They stared at each other in silence, while Gabrielle's heart raced. A smile trembled on her lips. She longed to fly across the corridor and throw herself into his arms, to kiss his mouth and caress his face.

The bodyguard mumbled something and touched her arm. Gabrielle shook free of his hand. 'James,' she said again, while tears rose in her eyes.

James's mouth twisted. Darkness grew within his pale eyes, and then he stepped away from his companion and moved towards her.

There were voices behind her. She heard footsteps, sensed Vitale's presence, and then his heavy arm was around her shoulders, his cologne was gagging her.

'Is this man bothering you, *cara mia*?'

His husky voice sounded casual, but Gabrielle knew him well. There was steel beneath his tone, just as there was in the press of his hand.

She didn't trust herself to speak. 'No,' she said finally, her eyes locked with James's, 'no. He—he...'

James looked at Vitale, and a chill cut into Gabrielle's heart. She had seen that look on his face before, the night the intruder had broken into the carriage house.

It was a look that said he was capable of anything.

'Let go of her,' he said softly.

Time hung in delicate balance. She felt Vitale tense, heard the shuffle of the bodyguard's feet.

James took a step forward. 'I said, let her go.'

His words were a silken warning. Vitale cleared his throat, looked around him at the plush surroundings of the opera house, and then his arm fell away from Gabrielle.

In one easy motion, James caught hold of her and drew her to him. She heard Vitale's muttered oath, knew she would pay a heavy penalty for this transgression, but it was impossible not to move into James's arms.

This one moment, captured from the web of time, was worth any risk.

A smile trembled on her lips. 'James,' she said again, and his arms closed tightly around her. She felt the hard press of his body against hers, smelled the clean essence that was his alone, and then his mouth was on hers.

But this kiss was unlike any they'd shared. James's lips ravaged hers, his teeth bit sharply into her flesh. Her mouth opened at the pressure and his tongue probed for admittance, mimicking the act of love, making it into an act of vengeance instead.

The radiant joy that had been within her heart fractured into a million crystalline shards. James despised her, as she'd known he must. Tears filled her eyes and trickled down her cheeks. The salty taste of them filled her mouth.

She thought she heard James groan. His mouth seemed to gentle on hers, and her heart leaped. She moved in his arms and he caught her even closer to him. Yes, she thought fiercely, yes...

He thrust her from him with an abruptness that made her gasp. Her eyes flew open; she stared at him as he wiped the back of his hand across his mouth, and then he gave her a smile so filled with hate that it drove the breath from her lungs.

'You can have her, Vitale,' he said. 'What the hell, I already had what I wanted.'

She fell back under the cruel lash of his words. Vitale's arm curved around her again. Tears rolled down her cheeks as he led her through the opera house and out to his waiting limousine. He handed her in and she curled into the far corner, her hands pressed to her mouth to stifle her sobs.

Vitale's rage was terrifying.

'That son of a bitch,' he muttered while the car sped through the dark streets, 'that bastard! I'll kill him. I'll cut off his——'

The cold promise in his voice roused her. 'No,' she said sharply, looking at his shadowy face. 'We made a deal, remember?'

He stared at her. 'He insulted me. No one does that and lives, Gabriella. No one.'

From somewhere came the strength to hold her head high and meet his threat with her own. 'If you touch him, I'll leave you.'

He laughed. 'How? You'll never get out the door.'

She drew in her breath. 'There are many ways to leave someone,' she said softly.

Silence fell between them, and then Vitale nodded stiffly. 'What the hell,' he said, 'let him live. You'll never see the bastard again anyway.'

Gabrielle lay her head back and closed her eyes. 'No,' she whispered, 'I never will.'

CHAPTER TWELVE

'YOUR gown is so beautiful, Signorina Chiari.' The young housemaid's voice bubbled with excitement. 'I've never seen a train so long, have you?'

Gabrielle turned in the window-seat and stared at the girl. 'No,' she said after a while, 'I suppose not.'

'And the garden—have you been downstairs to see it? All the little lights they put in the trees, and the umbrella tables, and...' She paused, then giggled softly. 'Aren't I silly? Of course you've seen it. Your window looks right out over everything.'

Gabrielle stared out of the glass again, and then she nodded. 'Everything,' she murmured. 'All the preparations for the circus.'

'For the...' The girl's eyebrows rose. 'Well, yes, it's going to be a big wedding, isn't it?' She ran her tongue across her lips and took a step towards Gabrielle. 'Rosa— Cook says there'll be two hundred people here tomorrow. Is that so?'

Gabrielle leaned her head back against the wall and closed her eyes. 'Ask Mr Vitale.' Her voice was dull. 'I don't know anything about it.'

'*Signorina?*' The girl hesitated. 'Are you ill?'

The young voice, so filled with excitement a moment ago, was taut with concern. It took effort to open her eyes and force a smile to her lips, but somehow Gabrielle managed.

'No,' she said gently, 'I'm fine.'

The girl's eyes moved across Gabrielle's face. 'Are you certain? You're very pale.'

Gabrielle nodded. 'I'm OK. Really.' She rose slowly and tightened the sash of her silk robe. 'Its been a long day, that's all. I need some rest.'

The maid blushed. 'Of course. Forgive me, *signorina*. You'll need all your energy for tomorrow.' She giggled again. 'It's not every day a woman gets married.'

The door closed quietly after the young woman, and Gabrielle sank to the window-seat again and looked out into the garden.

How festive it looked. Lights, tables, huge vases of flowers everywhere—a smile, a real one this time, moved, ghost-like, over her mouth.

Alma would never believe the flowers. Vitale had ordered things unheard of in this part of the world. Flowers had been shipped in from Hawaii, from the South Seas, some with names that were as exotic as their colour and foliage.

Alma. What was she doing on this warm June night? There'd been only some brief contact between them, once when Gabrielle wrote and told her she'd deeded the flower shop to her, again when Alma had written back, thanking Gabrielle for the unexpected gift. Her note had been polite, but beneath the very proper wording Gabrielle had sensed her friend's hurt.

'You could have told me the truth about yourself, Gaby,' Alma had written at the end. 'I thought I was your friend.'

Gabrielle sighed and got to her feet again. She had no friends, not any more. She had only Tony Vitale—and tomorrow, she would become his wife.

A rush of terrible images tumbled into her mind. She saw herself walking down the aisle towards a smiling Vitale, saw his mouth move over hers after the ceremony, saw herself moving through the afternoon, Vitale's arm around her waist, saw the door to his bedroom close after her and then—and then . . .

A tremor raced through her. How would she live through tomorrow and all the tomorrows that came after?

Quickly, Gabrielle stripped off her robe and got into bed. Sleep had become her benefactor, taking her from a reality she couldn't face to a dream-world of her own making. Sometimes, her dreams were of her childhood, when her father was the healthy, loving man she'd always known, and she'd awake with a smile on her lips.

More often, she dreamed of James—James as he had been during those few precious days they'd had together in New Orleans. She awakened smiling from those dreams, too, although her smile would fade quickly as reality rushed in.

But dreams were all she would have of the man she loved, and she welcomed them, no matter how unhappy the moment of awakening.

She sighed as her cheek touched the cool satin pillowcase. James, she thought, I love you. Even though you hate me, I'll always love you. Always.

But on this night, the dreams Gabrielle longed for evaded her. She thrashed in her bed, slipping from one troubled nightmare to another. And then, suddenly, she was wide awake, and a scream was rising in her throat.

There was a hand over her mouth, a man's hand. Her eyes widened as she looked up into the face leaning over her.

It was James. Her pulse began to race.

He smiled down at her in the moonlit dark. It was a smile that turned her blood to ice.

'That's right, baby,' he whispered. 'It's me.' His smile fled. 'And if you value your life, you won't make a sound.'

Gabrielle stared at him, stunned. How had he got into her room? For that matter, how had he got into the house? It should have been impossible to gain access to the Vitale compound. On her return from New Orleans, she'd noticed that electronic devices now controlled the gate and there were dogs, too, huge Rottweilers that were kept kennelled during the day and given the run of the place after dark.

'Get up—and be quick about it.'

'How—how did you get here? How...?'

He slid back the wardrobe doors that lined one wall and pulled something from the rack.

'Here, put this on,' he said, tossing it at her. The sable coat Vitale had bought her slithered towards her across the silk sheets. She sat up and stuffed her arms into the sleeves of the coat. The fur was a silly thing to wear on such a warm night, and she'd never liked it anyway— she felt a kinship with the agony of the animals who'd ended their lives in traps just as she was doomed to do. But she did as James ordered, then stuffed her feet into the high-heeled silk slippers that had been Vitale's idea, while her mind raced. What was happening?

'James. Please, you must tell me...'

He grasped her elbow and hurried her across the room. 'Just keep moving,' he whispered, pausing at the door. Her heart pounded as he cracked it open and peered into the hall. 'All right. Not a sound now, Gabrielle, I'm warning you.'

She hung back as he began opening the door. The hall was dimly lit; shadows hung in the corners and over the wide oak staircase. Someone would hear them. Vitale's men were everywhere in the house, and Big Tony himself slept only two doors away. They'd kill James if they found him here.

She pulled free of his hand. 'Do you know what Vitale will do when he catches us?' she whispered.

James's teeth glinted in the dark. '*If* he catches us. Don't worry, baby. You can always tell him I forced you to come with me. Now move.'

'He'll kill you,' she hissed. 'James, for the love of God...'

'Your concern touches me deeply,' he snarled, and he put his hand in the small of her back and began to propel her forward. 'Now move!'

'James, I beg you...'

His arm slid around her waist and he pulled her against him. The heat of his body was like a furnace. She felt her skin blaze beneath the weight of the fur.

'Listen to me.' His lips were against her ear; the warmth of his breath seemed to enter her blood. 'If you don't do exactly as I tell you, I'll wake this whole damned house. I'll tell Tony you arranged this meeting, that you slipped me a key to the gate.'

'Are you insane? He knows that's impossible. I have no...'

James laughed softly. 'Yes, I know. You have no wish to leave him or this place.' His arm tightened around her. 'But you'll never convince Big Tony of that. Not after what he saw that night at the opera.'

'What do you mean?' she said, trying to make sense of his words. She remembered their meeting and Vitale's rage afterwards. But James couldn't know about that.

'I can still make you want me,' he said hoarsely, 'and Vitale knows it.' He looked into her eyes. 'Shall I prove it to you?' His mouth dropped to hers, his kiss as hard as his words. Desire spiralled within her, rising up despite her fear, and she swayed towards him, her lips parting beneath the pressure of his. His kiss gentled as Gabrielle moved against him, and then suddenly he made a sound in the back of his throat and put her from him.

'James,' she whispered brokenly, 'James.'

His breath hissed between his teeth. 'Damn you,' he said. 'I ought to leave you here.'

Gabrielle caught her bottom lip between her teeth. Tears filled her eyes as she looked into the face of the only man she would ever love. His hatred for her blazed in his eyes.

'Yes,' she whispered, 'leave me here, James. Please. No one will ever know.'

His mouth narrowed. 'Wouldn't you love that?' His arm curved around her waist and he pulled the door open. 'OK. Here we go. Remember, not a sound or I'll toss you to the wolves.'

Or the dogs, she thought as they moved silently down the hall to the staircase. Nervous laughter rose in her throat and she swallowed hard, forcing it back. If James had got in without being attacked by the Rottweilers, he could get out. That was what she told herself, but she didn't really believe it.

She didn't believe they'd get through the front door, either, without alarms and bells blasting the night. But they did, and within seconds they were hurrying down the drive towards the gate. Gabrielle hardly dared breathe. She expected to hear the pad of the dogs' feet behind her or the shouted challenge of Vitale's men— but the compound was a silent shell.

Her heart began to race with excitement. The gate was just ahead. Even at a distance, she could see that it was open. She was free. Free! She was...

Who was she kidding? She could never be free. She had made a deal with Vitale and she would keep it. What was freedom compared to the knowledge that James was alive? It was the only thing that had kept her going these past months. If she stepped outside those gates, if she violated her part of the agreement...

She came to a stop. 'I can't. I can't leave Vitale.'

James spun towards her and spat a curse that was like a knife-thrust to the heart.

'Damn you,' he said, and he swung her up into his arms.

'Put me down. Please, James. Don't take me away. Don't!'

Struggling against him was useless. She felt helpless, just as she had the last night they'd been together.

She had been afraid then, but not as much as she was now. Then, she had feared for her own life.

Now, she feared for his.

There was a car waiting at the kerb. James set her down on the pavement while he opened the door, and then he pushed her into the passenger seat. Seconds later, the engine coughed and the car sped off into the night.

Ages seemed to pass until they pulled into a garage beneath an apartment building overlooking the East River. James took her arm as he led her to a bank of lifts. His touch was impersonal; she knew he was only holding her to keep her from running, and she wanted to tell him not to bother, it was too late to flee, there was no way she could slip back into Vitale's house now. Too much time had elapsed: they must know she was gone.

Why had James stolen her away? What had happened? Vitale's rage would be frightening. She knew he'd want to kill James, but there had to be a way to calm him long enough to make him realise that he would gain nothing by doing it.

He had her. He would always have her—so long as James was alive.

'Inside.'

She looked up, blinking as she realised they'd left the lift and were standing before an open door. Lights came on as she stepped inside, and the door slammed shut behind her.

They were in James's apartment. Gabrielle would have known that if she'd come here without him. His presence was everywhere, in the well-worn leather chairs that flanked a charcoal-grey couch, in the shelves filled with books, even in the gleaming hardwood floor that stretched to the wall of glass beyond.

The room was like him: big, masculine, without pretence. She thought of the pretension of the Vitale house and she smiled.

James moved past her, shrugging off his jacket and tossing it on the couch.

'Coffee or brandy?' he asked.

Gabrielle looked at him. 'Why did you bring me here?'

He looked at her, then turned to a cabinet built into one long wall. 'Brandy,' he said, taking down a pair of balloon goblets and a decanter filled with an amber liquid. He splashed brandy into the goblets, then handed one to her. 'Drink up.'

She raised the glass to her lips. The smell of the liquor was harsh, and she shook her head. 'Thank you, but——'

'Drink it.' His voice was rough. 'You need some colour in your cheeks.'

Her eyes met his, and the flat coldness of them made her shudder. 'All right,' she whispered, and she took an obedient swallow.

The brandy was strong. It exploded in her throat and she began to cough. James crossed the room to her.

'Easy,' he said, taking the glass from her hand and setting it down, 'just take a deep breath.' He tilted her face to his and looked at her. 'Are you OK?'

Gabrielle nodded. 'Yes.'

They stared at each other. A muscle ticked in his jaw, and she thought suddenly of the dark bruise that had once lay there. Her gaze swept up his face to his cheek. The scar from the car accident was barely visible, a thin white line angling across the tanned skin.

James. James, my love.

Her breath caught and she looked away. 'Yes,' she said again, and she managed a smile, 'I'm fine.'

James's hand spread along her cheek. 'You're not,' he said sharply. 'You've lost weight.' His fingers cupped her chin, lifting her face. 'There are shadows beneath your eyes.'

Gabrielle nodded. 'I—I haven't been sleeping well,' she said finally. 'I...'

I can't think, James. Not with your hand against my cheek, not when I can remember the taste of your skin. What would you do if I moved my head and pressed my lips to your palm?

A tremor went through her and she pulled free of his hand. 'I asked a question,' she said, moving away from him to the window. 'Why did you bring me here? And how did you get into the compound? The dogs—the alarm system...'

James shrugged his shoulders. 'I can't take any credit for putting either the dogs or the alarm out of commission. Federal agents did that. They took the Rottweilers out with drugs, the alarm with some kind of sophisticated technology.'

'But Vitale and his men were still in the house. They could have heard you. You could have been...'

'But I wasn't.' A quick smile twisted across his mouth. 'I counted on Vitale and his people sleeping like babies. Why wouldn't they, with a pack of guard dogs and a million-dollar electronic system to protect them?'

'I don't understand all this.'

He glanced at his watch. 'By now, your lover is in gaol. They busted him five minutes after I got you out of there tonight.'

'Busted?'

'Vitale's been arrested,' he said, watching her closely. 'They've been after him for months and I—they finally caught him with his hand in the cookie jar.'

Arrested. Vitale had been arrested. A feeling of hope energised her, but it was gone as swiftly as it had come. No gaol would hold Big Tony for long. He had the best legal advice money could buy, and no bail would be too high for him to meet.

And when he got out, he'd go looking for James— unless she could stop him.

Fear turned her blood cold. 'Where is he?' she said, brushing past him as she hurried towards the door. 'I have to go to him.'

James reached out as she moved past him and caught her by the sleeve. 'Damn you!' His voice was ragged. 'Can't you stay away from him for one night?'

Gabrielle looked at him. 'You don't understand,' she whispered. 'Please, James.'

His hands closed on her shoulders, his fingers imprinting themselves on her flesh even through the thickness of the sable coat.

'I was right about you all along,' he said, his eyes locked with hers. 'It wasn't that you didn't know the truth about Vitale—it was that you didn't care.'

'No. That's not——'

'He had money, that was all that mattered to you,' James said, shaking her like a sack of laundry. 'God, what panic you must have felt, Gabrielle. All those years of fancy living—the schools, the clothes, anything your little heart wanted—gone in a blink of an eye. You went to sleep a princess and woke up a commoner.'

She shook her head. 'It isn't true.'

His face twisted. 'Of course it's true,' he snarled. 'You and your old man had a good thing going. You had Big Tony wound around your little finger, and then Townsend and I came along and destroyed it.' He bent towards her, his eyes pale as moonlight. 'Choose, we said. Give up Vitale and protect your father, or hang on to Vitale and hand your old man over to us.'

'No. You're wrong. James, I beg you...'

He laughed. 'Hell, we did you a favour. I mean, we gave you the chance to use what passes for your heart for once in your life. You chose your father, even though protecting him meant kicking in the soft life with Vitale.'

Tears rose in Gabrielle's eyes. What had she expected him to think? Vitale had commanded a performance from her and she—she had done an award-winning job. The papers saw her as Vitale's woman; why wouldn't James think it, too? She had fled his arms and his love, she had flaunted everything they'd meant to each other.

James's lips curled as he watched the play of emotion on her face. 'I almost felt sorry for Vitale when he told me what happened that night he tried to have you killed.' He laughed. 'Not that he admitted that, of course. But——'

Gabrielle's eyes widened. 'You mean—you talked with him? When . . . ?'

'Didn't he tell you?' James smiled wolfishly. 'Hell, I thought he would. I figured the two of you would get a laugh out of it.' His grin vanished. 'Yeah, I talked to him. I pushed my way into his office one morning; I told him I wanted to see you, face to face, to have you tell me yourself that you'd gone back to him willingly.'

James had done that? He'd faced down Tony Vitale for her?

'He—he never said anything,' she said slowly. 'He never——'

His hands tightened on her. 'He told me how you phoned him while I was at the police station, how you begged to come back to him.'

She shook her head wildly. 'No. It's not true. I never——'

'And he decided to take you back. Hell, he's not stupid. He must have realised it was safer and cheaper to buy your silence than to have you killed.' His voice dropped to a chill whisper. 'Besides, why would he want you in a coffin when he could have you in his bed?'

Gabrielle drew a shuddering breath. 'James,' she whispered, 'please, you must listen to me. I—it wasn't like that. Vitale wasn't . . . I never . . .'

James looked at her as her words trailed away. 'Go on,' he said coldly, 'I'm listening. What lies are you going to tell me now?'

Her eyes met his. What could she say to him? Could she tell him the truth? Could she say, 'I love you, James'? No. She could never tell him that. If he knew what she'd done, the sacrifice she'd made, he would go after Vitale. That he'd sought him out once already in the past months was proof enough.

And then Vitale would kill him. *That* was the truth, the only one that mattered.

Gabrielle swallowed drily. 'No lies,' she whispered, her eyes meeting his. 'I—I'll tell you the truth.' Her heart stopped beating; she felt it frozen in her breast while she gathered her strength for what had to be said. 'It—it was all the way you said it was. I—I called Vitale after you left that night. I told him—I told him I knew he'd never meant to hurt me, that—that things had gotten out of hand...'

James's hands slid from her shoulders, moving slowly to her throat. They spread beneath the open neckline of the sable coat, his fingers warm and solid against the rapid flutter of her pulse.

'You sold yourself to him, didn't you?' His voice caught, then broke. 'Your body and your vow of silence for his money.'

'No,' she whispered, and then she took a deep breath. 'Yes,' she said, her eyes meeting his.

His fingers slid beneath the ruby necklace. 'Your warm mouth traded for these cold stones,' he said, his eyes never leaving hers. Suddenly, his hand curled around the necklace and he ripped it from her throat. It fell to the floor, the rubies sparkling like drops of blood against the wood.

Gabrielle blinked back her tears. 'Is—is that why you brought me here?' she whispered. 'So you could humiliate me?'

He laughed, and the sound tore at her heart. 'Is that what you think?'

'You knew they were going to raid the house and arrest Tony. You knew that would give you time to—to confront me. I don't—I don't blame you. But...'

James's mouth twisted. 'But?'

'But I...' Her voice broke. 'I wish you'd finish this, James. I can't—I can't...'

Tears began to roll down her cheeks. She couldn't stand much more of this. In a moment, she'd fling her arms around him and kiss away the angry furrows beside his mouth, brush away the deep grooves between his brows, she would tell him how much she loved him, and that would be as good as signing his death sentence.

'No, you don't want me to finish this.' His voice was grating. 'You don't, Gabrielle. You...'

His hands closed on the sable coat and he ripped it from her shoulders. The dark fur puddled at her feet like a chrysalis. James stared at her, his eyes moving slowly over the high-necked silk nightgown she wore, lingering at the thrust of her breasts and the curve of her belly. She felt her flesh bloom beneath the heat of his gaze.

'James,' she whispered.

Her arms lifted slowly to him. No, she thought, you mustn't. But she was moving towards him, her eyes on his face. He wanted to make love to her, she could see it in the masked tension that transformed his features. But it wasn't love, not any more. If he took her, it would be in anger, it would be an act of cold possession. He would take her for the same reasons he'd kissed her at the opera house—lust would mix with the need to stamp his brand on her as he thought Vitale had.

It would be an act of revenge, not love.

But she wanted him so badly; she wanted to feel the warmth of his mouth and the hardness of his body one last time, and then—and then she would flee into the night, she'd find Vitale and do whatever she had to do to win James's life, she'd plead and beg, she'd even abase herself and seduce him if that was what it took.

'James,' she sighed, her mouth inches from his.

He made a desperate choked sound, grasped her shoulders, and flung her from him. Her eyes flew open; she watched, stunned, as he snatched up her coat and wrapped it around her.

'Get out,' he said in a harsh whisper.

'No. No—please, not yet. I beg you.'

'Take a taxi back to the compound and pack whatever you can. Your furs, your jewels—if you know where Vitale keeps his cash, take that, too. Whatever you lay your hands on is going to have to last you a lifetime.'

What was he saying? Did he think he could order her away from New York? He couldn't; his welfare depended on her staying.

'I'm not leaving, James. When Vitale gets out...'

He threw back his head and laughed. 'I hate to disappoint you, love, but you're not going to be able to rely on Tony any more.' His laughter faded and his eyes cut into her. 'You're going to have to fall back on your own resources, Gabrielle, but hell, that shouldn't be a problem for a woman like you.'

Gabrielle stared at him. 'What do you mean?'

James walked across the room and poured himself another dollop of brandy. 'All right,' he said, 'why not? You might as well hear it all.' He tilted the glass to his lips and tossed down the fiery liquid. 'Hell, I've already made a fool of myself—why shouldn't you have the last laugh?'

He slammed the glass down on a table; the fragile stem snapped, then broke, and a drop of amber liquid spilled on to the wood. He turned to her, his eyes burning with dark night fires.

'I quit the prosecutor's office. Did you know that?'

She nodded. 'Vitale told me.'

'Hell, when I took that job I was so damned self-righteous. I told my father I was going to be the kind of lawyer he wasn't.'

'I don't understand. What does your father have to do with this?'

'My father practises corporate law. He asked me to come into his firm with him, but I was such a smug bastard, accusing him of believing in nothing but dollar signs. I was going to save the world.' He walked to the window and put his palms against it, staring out into the night and the lights winking across the river in the borough of Queens. 'After a few years, I got my first big case. The authorities had been after Tony Vitale for years, and they finally had something on him.'

'The killing of Riley,' Gabrielle said softly.

James nodded. 'Yes. But we needed your testimony to make murder charges stick.' He paused; she saw his shoulders rise as he drew a deep breath. 'I was determined to find a way to force you to co-operate.' He leaned his forehead against the glass. 'And I did. But along the way—along the way, I learned some ugly truths. I learned that I don't have a lock on morality, that life isn't as black and white as I wanted it to be.' He drew in his breath again, then turned towards her. 'And I learned I could fall in love with a woman who represented everything I claimed to despise.'

Gabrielle's heart filled with love. If only she could go to him. If only she could tell him...

'By the time your father died, I hated myself for what I'd done to you. I knew your life was in danger—I wanted to protect you...'

'So you followed me to New Orleans.'

James nodded. 'Yes. I told myself it was only to safeguard you as a future witness. But it was more than that...' He fell silent. When he spoke again, his voice was low. 'When I came back to the carriage house that night and found you'd gone, I almost went crazy. I drove the streets of the Quarter, I searched the city—I demanded the cops send out an all-points bulletin. But then, the next day, your picture was everywhere. You and Vitale...'

Gabrielle closed her eyes. She and Vitale, the photo of her in his arms, his wet mouth against hers.

'I wanted to kill you both. I dreamed about it; hell, I even...' He paused and drew a breath. 'In the end, I decided there had to be a better way.' His head lifted and he looked at her. 'I decided to put Tony Vitale away. Forever.'

'You can't,' she whispered. 'No one can.'

James gave her a bitter smile. 'I hate to disappoint you, baby. I took a logic course in college once—I've forgotten most of it, but one thing impressed the hell out of me. There aren't any insoluble problems, just poor solutions. So I stopped concentrating on the Riley murder and I took a good, hard look at all the other slime Vitale's involved in.'

She stared at him, afraid to ask the question. Finally, she cleared her throat.

'And did you—did you find something?'

'No,' he said, and her heart plummeted. What had she expected? Vitale was careful; look how many years it had taken her to see the truth about him. But James was still talking, and suddenly she realised he was telling her he'd found nothing he could use—at first. And then, suddenly, he'd turned up a lead.

'Townsend wouldn't touch it; there wasn't enough to go on. So I quit my job and I went out on my own, listening to anybody who'd talk, buying whatever information I could—and then, last week, it all came together.'

She stared at him, her heart beginning to trip erratically, afraid to let herself believe.

'I don't suppose...' Her voice faded and she inhaled shakily. 'I don't suppose you found what you'd been looking for, though.' She hesitated. 'A way to—to put him away forever.'

James looked at her. 'I hope you've managed to put aside something for a rainy day, baby.' His eyes were stones. 'Although you've probably got enough on your back right now to last a lifetime.'

'James,' she whispered, 'please—tell me. Did you...?'

His lips drew back from his teeth. 'I did, indeed. Vitale's hands are so dirty, he'll spend the rest of his life in prison and never get them clean.'

Gabrielle began to tremble. 'Are you sure?'

'That's what tonight's arrest was all about.' His mouth twisted with pain. 'I struck a deal with Townsend—I convinced him to let me get you out first, although why in hell I did it...' He turned away from her and looked out of the window. 'Come on,' he said with a terrible weariness in his voice, 'I'll get you a taxi.'

She was dizzy with excitement. Was it true? Had James's rage worked in a way he'd never intended? Had it set her free? It seemed too much to believe, and yet...

She took a hesitant step towards him. 'James? Are you certain? Vitale will—he'll never get out of prison?'

He shook his head. 'Not in this lifetime, he won't.' Suddenly, he spun towards her. 'What's the matter, Gabrielle? Are you afraid you won't be able to...?' The angry tumble of words stopped when he saw her face. 'What are you smiling at?' he demanded.

Her smiled faded. He was looking at her with such cold fury—would he believe her story? Would he even listen while she told it?

'James.' Her voice was a tremulous whisper. She held her hand out to him, as if to implore his understanding. 'I—I have something to tell you.'

He watched her through narrowed eyes. 'And I'll just bet it's fascinating.' His words fell between them like bits of ice.

Gabrielle swallowed. 'I—I didn't go back to Vitale willingly. He forced me.'

She waited, her breath stilled. Something gleamed in his eyes, then was snuffed out. 'As I said, fascinating.' He turned away. 'Let's go. It's getting late.'

'James.' Desperation gave her courage, and she took a step forward again. 'Please, you must listen.' She watched his back, the stiffness in his shoulders, the rigidity of his spine. 'That night—Vitale telephoned me after you left. He said if I didn't come back to him, he'd—he'd kill you. So...'

He turned to face her, his face white and pinched. 'What the hell kind of fool do you take me for?' he demanded. 'The cop on duty at your front door told me how you'd called him inside to check on a noise, how you'd sneaked out while he was upstairs——'

'He lied. Vitale arranged it. He arranged for my plane ticket, for the cab that picked me up——'

James's mouth curled in disgust. 'Stop lying, damn you! It's over. You've lost, don't you see that? Just be grateful you still have the things he gave you, the furs and the jewels and...'

'The things he gave you.' That was what he believed, that Vitale had bought her. She thought back, remembering his bitter words when they first met, the questions about how she'd gotten the carriage house in New Orleans, the suggestions that it had been hard to turn away from the man who'd given her presents back in New York.

Nothing that had happened since would have convinced him that he'd been wrong. There'd been pictures of her everywhere, stories about the fortune in jewels and furs Vitale had lavished on her. Even now, as she pleaded with James to believe her, she was draped in Big Tony's booty, wearing his silks and furs and gems.

Her glance fell to the ruby necklace lying on the floor, and a sudden hope was kindled in her heart.

'Those windows,' she said slowly, looking at the wall of glass that looked out over the river, 'do they open?'

James frowned. 'If you're warm, take off that damned coat. Surely you can be separated from it for a few minutes?'

She bent and picked up the ruby necklace. Her fingers curled around it as she moved past him to the window and looked out. Far below, the river gleamed like black oil beneath the lights of New York City.

'Do they open?' she repeated.

James sighed. 'Yes,' he said, and he slid a glass panel aside. Warm summer air, rich with the smells of the city and the ocean beyond, blew into the room. 'Are you satisfied now?'

Gabrielle smiled. 'I love you,' she said. 'I've never loved anyone but you.'

His face paled beneath its tan. 'Don't lie,' he said roughly. 'It isn't... God!' His voice rose in shock. 'What the hell are you doing?'

Her smile broadened as the ruby necklace fell through the night, twinkling like hundreds of tiny suns as it rushed to the waiting river. James stared at her in disbelief, and she laughed a little.

'Tiffany's,' she said. 'Two hundred and seventy-five thousand dollars. Can you imagine that?' Her eyes held his as she slipped a ruby and sapphire bracelet from her wrist. 'This is from Bulgari. Twenty thousand, I think.' She laughed again, this time at the look on his face. 'Well, maybe just a little bit more.' Her arm drew back, her hand flexed, and the bracelet soared out of the window, winked against the inky darkness, and vanished from sight.

James took a step towards her. 'Gabrielle. What are you doing?'

'And then, of course, there's this.' She pulled the diamond ring from her finger and held it before her. Held in her palm, the huge stone looked even more vulgar than usual. 'I hated this most,' she said with a shudder. 'God, how I hated it!' A quick toss, and the ring sailed after the bracelet, winking like a shooting star as it tumbled through the sky.

'Gabrielle.' James's voice was hoarse. 'Do you know what you're doing? I told you, Vitale's never going to see daylight again. He——'

'Are you sure?'

He nodded, and she laughed aloud. 'I almost forgot these,' she said, plucking the diamond clips from her ears. 'Ten thousand dollars—isn't that obscene?'

The earrings caught the light as they hurtled out of the window, tumbling over and over like tiny planets rushing to oblivion.

James put out his hand, then let it fall to his side. 'Listen to me. You're throwing away everything. There won't be any more, don't you understand? Vitale——'

'Will never get out of prison.' She smiled. 'Yes, I know.'

'Then what are you doing?'

'Last, but certainly not least...' She shrugged off the sable coat, stepping free of it as it fell gracefully to the floor. James stared at it, and then his eyes met hers. She smiled. 'Actually, I hate to send the coat to a watery grave. I mean, why should all those little animals have died in vain?'

James shoved his hand through his hair. The look on his face brought a bubble of laughter to her throat. 'All right, that's enough. Tell me what...'

She cocked her head, and her hair slipped across the silk of her nightgown. 'What do you think—the coat, I mean. If we took it to a charity, could they find a use for it?'

James swallowed hard. 'What is this?' he whispered, his eyes narrowing as they focused on her. 'What kind of game...?'

She moved slowly towards him, stopping when she was a hand's distance away.

'No game,' she said softly. She lifted her arms slowly and put them around his neck. His body stiffened beneath her touch. 'I love you, James. I've loved you from the beginning.' A smile tilted at her mouth. 'Well, not that morning in the alley. You scared the life out of me then.'

James's arms rose, then fell to his sides. 'You're only saying that because Vitale's going to be locked up for the rest of his life.'

Gabrielle nodded. 'That's absolutely right.' His eyes grew dark, and she sighed and put her hand to his face, smoothing away the lines in his forehead. 'It wouldn't be safe to tell you otherwise.'

'What's that supposed to mean?' he growled.

'Vitale said he'd kill you if I didn't go to him.' She watched his face, waiting for some sign that he believed her, but it was like watching a mask. 'I swear it,' she whispered.

A muscle knotted in James's jaw. 'Dammit, Gabrielle, if this is some kind of game...'

She rose on tiptoe and pressed her mouth lightly to his. 'I love you, James.' Still, he said nothing. Tears filled her eyes and gleamed on her dark lashes. 'I even loved you the night I thought you'd been sent to kill me.'

James groaned softly. 'Gabrielle.' His arms closed around her with a ferocity that drove the breath from her lungs. 'My love,' he whispered. 'How could you have thought such a thing?'

A dizzying rush of happiness swept through her. She lay her head against his shoulder, revelling in the feel of him in her arms.

'How could you have believed I'd leave you for Tony Vitale?'

'I don't know,' he said slowly. 'Equal parts stupidity and blindness, I guess.'

She leaned back in his arms and smiled. 'You see? We were both dumb.'

James smiled, and then his mouth narrowed to a thin line. 'That bastard,' he said. 'Forcing you to go to him, imprisoning you . . .'

'Hush.' She kissed him lightly on the mouth. 'I'd have gone to the ends of the earth for you, James. I'm just glad there was a way to keep you alive.'

He drew her close to him. She could feel the race of his heart against hers.

'Can you forgive me for ever doubting you?' he whispered.

Gabrielle sighed. 'I told you, we were both foolish.' She drew back and smiled at him. 'But people in love aren't known for logic.'

'Sometimes they are,' he said, and then he kissed her, gently at first, then with a passion that dazzled her senses. When he raised his head, he was smiling. 'For instance—only a logical man would interrupt this long enough to ask for your hand in marriage.'

Gabrielle laughed softly. 'And only a logical woman would take time to accept.' She kissed his neck, then leaned back in his arms and looked into his eyes. 'Alma would approve of that proposal, sir. It was very sweet and old-fashioned.'

James's eyes darkened. 'I like old-fashioned things,' he murmured. 'Like this nightgown you're wearing. How do these buttons open?'

She sighed as she guided his hands. 'Easily,' she whispered. 'Let me show you.'

High over the East River, the sun rose blazing into the morning sky.

Harlequin Presents®

Coming Next Month

Available in April wherever paperback books are sold, or through Harlequin Reader Service:

In the U.S.
P.O. Box 1397
Buffalo, N.Y.
14240-1397

In Canada
P.O. Box 603
Fort Erie, Ontario
L2A 5X3

Coming soon
to an easy chair near you.

FIRST CLASS is Harlequin's armchair travel plan for the incurably romantic. You'll visit a different dreamy destination every month from January through December without ever packing a bag. No jet lag, no expensive air fares and *no* lost luggage. Just First Class Harlequin Romance reading, featuring exotic settings from Tasmania to Thailand, from Egypt to Australia, and more.

FIRST CLASS romantic excursions guaranteed! Start your world tour in January. Look for the special **FIRST CLASS** destination on selected Harlequin Romance titles—there's a new one every month.

NEXT DESTINATION:
GREECE

 Harlequin Books

JTR4

COMING IN 1991 FROM
HARLEQUIN SUPERROMANCE:

Three abandoned orphans,
one missing heiress!

Dying millionaire Owen Byrnside receives an
anonymous letter informing him that twenty-six years
ago, his son, Christopher, fathered a daughter. The
infant was abandoned at a foundling home that
subsequently burned to the ground, destroying all
records. Three young women could be Owen's long-
lost granddaughter, and Owen is determined to track
down each of them! Read their stories in

#434 HIGH STAKES (available January 1991)
#438 DARK WATERS (available February 1991)
#442 BRIGHT SECRETS (available March 1991)

Three exciting stories of intrigue and romance by
veteran Superromance author Jane Silverwood.